THE DOUBLE CROSS

BY

C. David Claybrook

No part of this book may be reproduced, stored in a retrieval system, or transmitted by any means without the written permission of the publisher.

Copyright © 2020 LifeWorks LLC. All rights reserved.

INTRODUCTION

A few years back, I had the wonderful privilege of taking a tour of Israel, the Holy Land. We traveled to many sites throughout the country. We were blessed to be able to walk the streets of old Jerusalem and we visited several sites including Calvary and the Garden of Gethsemane. The descriptions in this book are taken from those experiences.

One unexpected stop was the home of Caiaphas, the High Priest during the days of Jesus. Like maybe all in our tour group, I was completely surprised to learn about the underground dungeon in Caiaphas' house. While looking around in that prison I began to wonder, *"What if Jesus and Barabbas had been here at the same time? What would have happened between them?"*

The mental image of that possible encounter was the seed that later grew into the story of *THE DOUBLE CROSS*.

If you are able, when finished, please take a few minutes and go online and write a review of this book. I look forward to reading what you have to say and possibly how future editions can be improved.

                              Thank you,

                          C. David Claybrook

Chapter One

"This way Jonah, back there!" The older man pulled the younger man behind a huge stone.

"Put your weight against it. We have to move this."

"This thing is heavy," Jonah complained as he began to push against the boulder.

"Quit griping!" the older man, Rab, said as he pushed in beside Jonah. "Move over. Make room for me."

With both putting their weight against the stone, it began to move slightly.

"Keep pushing."

Finally the stone was moved enough to reveal an opening in the stone pavement and several stone steps descending into a dark tunnel.

Pointing to Jonah's right, Rab said, "See those broken branches over there? Go get them and we will use them to cover this entrance after we go down,"

As Jonah dragged the browned limbs, Rab very carefully started down the steps into the tunnel. Jonah turned and backed down the steps pulling the branches over the hole after him. He looked behind him to see where he was going, but the sunlight only went so far into the shaft. He turned and sat down on a step. After a minute, he reached out to touch both side walls, stood up and then continued to descend feeling with his feet for each step. After more than a dozen steps he came to level ground and moved forward in the pitch black. After a few steps he bumped into Rab.

"Did you get the hole covered?" Rab asked as he slumped down onto the floor.

"The best I could," Jonah said as he dropped down beside Rab.

They blinked as their eyes adjusted from the bright sunlight of the Jerusalem spring afternoon to the darkness of the tunnel. The men were breathing heavily, winded by their sprints to safety and the struggle with the huge stone. Both shuddered in the cool, damp air but held their breaths long enough to listen for any sign their pursuers had seen them enter the underground passage.

"Wow! That was amazing!" Jonah was finally able to speak between pants. "Did anyone see us?"

"I don't think so, but we can't sit here long. Did you see what happened to Isaac?" Rab asked.

"The last time I saw him he was lying on the ground. He must have fallen or something. They probably caught him." Cursing, he continued, "I sure hope he knows how to keep his mouth shut."

"Come on, we've got to get going," Rab said as he pushed himself up and turned toward the darkness. He had only taken one step when Jonah grabbed his arm and said, "I can't see a thing. Where are we going?"

Rab jerked his arm free and said, "You can reach both sides of this small tunnel. Touch them if you must or just stay close behind me. We have got to get moving."

"Rab, what is this place?" the young man asked as he followed behind, trying to stay as close as possible without stepping on the older man's feet.

"Shhh! Keep your voice down, Jonah. Sound really travels down here."

"Well, what is it?" Jonah asked again, his agitation showing even in his forced whisper.

"It's one of the tunnels under the city," Rab explained. "I don't know a lot about history, but I do know there are several of these tunnels down here. I think this one was built by King Hezekiah."

"King Hezekiah? Who is that?"

"I'm not sure, but the story that I heard was that the water from the underground springs on the other side of the city had been directed to flow out to areas outside the walls to provide water for the farmers in the nearby valley. Sometime while Hezekiah was our king, the King of Assyria invaded with a huge army. He started up north and conquered several cities. Hezekiah knew that he would then come and lay siege to Jerusalem. To keep the enemy army from having access to the water, Hezekiah ordered that a second wall be built outside the springs and a series of tunnels be dug underground to divert the water into the city. This is one of those tunnels."

Even though he could see nothing, Rab had been shuffling along at a fair pace, just guiding himself by touching both sides of the very narrow tunnel. Jonah had dropped back a bit to keep from continually bumping into his leader and he, too, was touching the sides of what seemed to him like a very narrow cave.

"Where does this lead?" Jonah asked.

"I hope this one leads to the Pool of Siloam."

"You hope. What does that mean?" Jonah could barely contain his frustration; or was it fear?

"Well over the years there have been more tunnels added to distribute the water to more of the city, but wherever we come out it will be in the old part of the city, away from the crowds ... and the soldiers I hope."

For what seemed like an eternity to Jonah they shuffled along, quiet except for their heavy breathing and the rhythm of their sandals on the stone floor.

"You said this goes to the Pool of Siloam?" Jonah asked.

Rab just grunted.

"If that's the case, shouldn't there be water flowing in here?"

"Not in this part of the tunnel, but when we get a little further, we will have to start wading in the water."

"No!" Jonah started to protest. "It's bad enough to be who knows where, down here in complete darkness. Now, you are telling me we are going to have to get wet."

"Would you rather get damp or get dead?' Rab snarled.

"What do you mean?"

"We could choose to go through one of the other sections…" Rab began.

"And then what?" Jonah interrupted.

"We get lost and likely no one will ever find us."

Just as he said that Rab suddenly stopped. Jonah ran into his back, but Rab did not react.

"Listen, do you hear that?" Rab asked.

Jonah listened. "It sounds like water running. Is it?"

"Yes, we are getting close."

Almost immediately Rab stepped down into a little deeper channel and felt the flow of the water.

"Here we go! We will follow the stream down to the pool of Siloam. It won't be that far now."

"Man, this water is cold," Jonah grumbled.

After what seemed another long time, the two turned a corner and could then see a dull glow of light reflecting on the water ahead.

"We're almost there. Let's be careful that we don't attract too much attention as we go out by the pool."

They turned another corner and a brilliant shaft of sunlight burst into the passageway. After allowing his eyes to adjust, Rab leaned against the tunnel wall and said to Jonah, "You stay here. I'm going to look to see what's going on out there. I'll be right back."

Rab hunched over, took a few steps and peered through the opening, looking one way and then the other. There were a fairly large number of people with skins getting water from the pool. Fortunately they seemed to be busy with the water and/or interacting with others. None seemed to notice Rab as he peeked out from the tunnel. Best of all: No soldiers!

Rab slipped back inside and turned back to Jonah who

had pulled his robe up and was wringing it out.

"Now look. I don't know what happened to Isaac and so we'd better not take any chances. If they got him, he will talk. They have ways of making a man talk. You need to get out of town. Go back to Bethlehem. I'm going to do the same, but we had better split up. We will meet at the usual place in two days. We can divide the gold there," he said as he held up the small sack of coins he had carried in his hand so they would not rattle as they had walked.

"What are the chances Isaac got away too?" Jonah looked up hopefully into the eyes of his leader. "I knew that old man was trouble. We should never have ..."

"That's enough! I don't want to hear it! It was my decision! Understand?" Rab snapped.

He could barely see the young man's eyes in the sparse light, but he knew the look of disgust they communicated ... and the truth. This had been his operation and as far as he could tell, the little bit of gold they had taken was not worth the trouble they had gone to or the chances they had taken. If Isaac had been captured, sooner or later he would talk. By that time, both Jonah and he needed to be far away from Jerusalem. They might even need to leave Judea.

"Come on, get going."

Jonah, squinting his eyes, stepped out first with Rab now following.

"Act casual, like you belong here like anyone else," Rab said quietly but loud enough to be heard over the rushing water. They moved through the crowd around the pool and on to the street. Hoping to appear normal and alone, the older man crossed over to the far side of the small cobblestone street and turned east, staying close to the white stone houses that lined the small street, which looked more like an alley. Jonah immediately turned the same direction, but stayed on the near side of the street. As they reached the first corner some twenty or so paces away, Rab looked over his shoulder to check the progress of his young partner. He was stunned to see that Jonah had walked directly into a squad of Temple soldiers who must have been approaching from a side street.

Where did they come from? Were they hiding in wait?

Before his mind had time to answer these questions, he felt a sharp pain at the base of his skull. He saw a brilliant burst of light and then everything went black.

Chapter Two

"Shut up, old man! We're sick of your crazy ranting."

The younger prisoner looked to his right in the direction of the older one, but could not see him. The dungeon in which they were being held was completely below ground level, under a house in fact. Its wicked construction allowed absolutely no light to penetrate the darkness. The only sensations that connected men condemned to this place with the real world were those inflicted upon the body: pain, the audible interchanges among the prisoners, and an occasional sound from the outside, filtered through the thick stone ceiling. And, of course there was the ever-present smell of human waste.

Everyone lost track of time, but they figured out that night and day could be distinguished by the activity of the guards. Brief glimpses of daylight would steal into the dungeon with the guards who, with torches in hand, came only to feed the prisoners, give them drink and, on rare occasion, to wash their refuse down into a crude and less than effective drainage system. The guards rarely came at all at night.

One would imagine that the souls of the prisoners would be as dark as their surroundings, but that was far from true. While they were angry at their captors and themselves for being stupid enough to have been caught in their misdeeds, thieves and murderers alike knew that as long as they were in this place they would again see the light of day. It was common knowledge that the nation's judicial system did not allow capital punishment and so though it might take months or even years, every prisoner believed he would eventually be freed. And so in this place, there was no atmosphere of morbidity, just frustration and hate!

"Isaac, I told you to shut up! It's your fault we're in here, and if you don't stop talking about God or Jesus or whatever it is that has got into your mind, I'm going to come over there and shut you up for good. You better hear what I am saying to you!" the young man shouted into the darkness. After a pause, he added, "No one is listening to you, not the priests upstairs, and not God in heaven."

If there is a god, He completed His tirade to Himself.

The younger man was Jonah, and as usual, his words betrayed the error of his thinking. He was wrong on almost every point. First, Isaac was not old, but forty seemed ancient to a man half that age. Neither was he crazy, nor ranting. At more than one time in his life, Isaac had actually seen God, and angels, and he definitely was praying or something as close to it as he knew how. Finally, Jonah was not going anywhere or going to shut anyone up. He could not because he was shackled, in a standing position, spread-eagle between two of the four columns that lined one side of the underground hallway that divided the main part of the prison into two cells. He was facing away from the hallway toward the back wall, though the darkness prevented him from seeing it. Isaac was in the same condition, his arms and legs drawn tight between two other columns, not six feet away. Chains kept Jonah from fulfilling his threat.

The third prisoner had fallen asleep and hung by his chains between his two partners in crime. His arms were stretched taunt and his legs sagged. His feet scrapped on the rough-hewn stones worn smooth over the years by the feet of men who had dared to violate God's law and had been foolish enough to get caught.

On the last two points, the twenty year old had been partially correct. He was right about the fact that the men upstairs definitely could not, would not hear the pleas of the old thief. It was the holiday season in Jerusalem, the capitol of the nation of Israel, and the high officials in the court of the land were preparing to take their honored seats at the Feast of Passover. They were not about to take time to hear the pleas of common criminals. But God was listening, even if Isaac and Jonah were unaware. And Jonah was wrong about Isaac being the reason they got caught. It was true, the forty year old had been the newest addition to the small gang, and he had been caught first. But whether Jonah believed it or not, he had not talked.

The sleeping man in the middle was the leader of their little gang. Rab, as he was called, was thirteen years Jonah's senior. He was also Jonah's hero. Jonah had looked up to Rab ever since he had decided not long after being declared a man at his Bar-Mitzvah that he knew more than his parents or teachers regarding how things worked in this world. He had liked the way Rab handled himself on the streets of their home town, Bethlehem. Rab was tough, self-assured, and in need of no one. Jonah wanted to be just like him.

Rab, a descendent of the tribe of Levi, had lived on the streets of Bethlehem since he was orphaned as a child. He could not remember a time when he did not know how to steal food or the silver needed to buy it. Nor could he remember a time when he did not have to. In his childhood, his intense feelings for the Romans, who occupied his homeland, had grown from fear to pure hatred. As a child he learned it was soldiers who had killed his family. He had just assumed they were Roman soldiers. By the time he learned they actually had been soldiers of Herod, the Jewish king, seeking to kill a child who was prophesied to be a new King of the Jews, his hatred was fixed on the foreigners.

Besides, he reasoned, *Herod was just a puppet of the Roman Caesar.*

He also had no use for God or the religious leaders who supposedly represented Him. He was told that his father had been such a man, a rabbi. In fact the thief's name, Barabbas, meant *Son of the Teacher* or *Son of the Father*. As an orphan Rab had not attended school long enough to learn much from the religious books. He did know some of the history of his people and he had heard of men like Abraham, Joseph, Moses and Joshua. Rab's given name was Jesus, which was a popularized form of Joshua, which in his native Hebrew meant *The LORD is Salvation.* It was a very common name, but needing some sense of purpose, when Rab first learned its meaning, he determined to make it his destiny. And so, like the Joshua of old, he intended to do all in his power to free his land from enemy occupation. Thus he preferred to be called Joshua, but like most everything else in his life, he did not get his way. Everyone called him Rab.

In order to survive as a child, Rab began a life of thievery. At thirty-three, he was little more than a common criminal, though he saw himself as a freedom fighter, a patriot. At the age of twenty he had taken the secret blood oath of the extremist underground resistance movement known as the Zealots. They were obliged to use any and all means possible to free their Jewish homeland from the domination of the hated Romans. This included killing any Roman soldier who happened to forget, if only for a moment, that he was the enemy of these fiercely independent people.

Rab's first "freedom act" had come quickly. Doing all he could to hold his teenage emotions in check in the midst of a crowd swollen by one of the three annual national festivals, he had eased up behind a soldier who had dropped behind his partner to examine some merchandise in a narrow street. In a motion made almost mechanical through practice, Rab had pulled a dagger from the sleeve of his tunic and plunged it violently between the ribs of the young soldier's back.

Under his breath, the young assassin had declared, *That's for my father.*

The soldier had not reacted immediately and Rab had disappeared into the crowd before the man realized the pain in his back was not from the normal jostling of the shoppers. His sudden drop to the ground created a commotion that brought a companion soldier running. Rab had watched from a safe distance as a squad of Roman soldiers gathered to offer assistance and to interrogate the bystanders. Neither enterprise proved fruitful.

At first Rab had kept count, one soldier for each of his slain family, but though that number had long since been completed, his vow had not been. He would be freed from his covenant of blood only when Israel was freed from Rome and had a king of its own, a real king, not a puppet like Herod. Rab reasoned that his life of rebellion would end when he bowed his knee before a new King of the Jews.

Rab now slept, in spite of Isaac's chanting and Jonah's ranting. He could sleep anywhere and just about had at one time or another. He needed the sleep to rest his mind as much as his body. This bit of sleep would give him some respite from his frustration. He, like Jonah, was completely incensed that he was in prison. Not that he had not been before, but the timing was the worst possible. It was the beginning of Passover, the week-long festival celebrating the Israelite's escape from slavery to the Egyptians hundreds of years before.

This was one of the few history stories Rab knew. The prophet Moses had succeeded in obtaining his ancestors' freedom from Pharaoh when a death angel from God killed the first born of every household in Egypt. Only those who had placed the blood of a slain lamb on their door posts had been exempt. The angel of death passed over the houses with the blood on the doors.

Rab was no more sentimental than he was religious. He cared little about the history or the feast, but he was an opportunist. Annually, the city swelled in population as thousands of Jews came from the known world to celebrate the Passover. Some were pious, but many came for the holiday atmosphere. It didn't matter much to Rab why they came as long as they came and brought their money bags full of gold and silver coins. He had also long since quit caring that Caesar's image was on most of the coins.

Crowds not only meant gold, they also meant more Roman soldiers in town. That is because the Roman governor always came down from his headquarters in Caesarea to attend the festival. Naturally he brought his own body guard for personal protection and to assist with crowd control. The added show of force naturally meant more danger to criminals, common thugs and Zealots alike, but as far as Rab was concerned the greater the challenge, the sweeter the success.

But success had alluded him this time, and unless the miracle Isaac was praying for happened, he and his gang were going to spend the festival days away from the foolish crowds, locked up in prison. The frustrating thing was that he had not been apprehended by the Romans for taking his revenge. He had not even had a chance. No! Jonah, Isaac and he had been caught by the Temple guards, of all people. These were Jewish soldiers whose duty was to police the Temple area. The Romans sanctioned this quasi-military force under the command of the Jewish High Priest. By doing so, Rome gave the appearance of respecting Jewish religion and law. But it was only in appearance. Jewish law dictated the death penalty of stoning for certain crimes. The Romans reserved for themselves the power to put men to death. They allowed the High Priest and the Sanhedrin, the Jewish High Court, to enforce only lesser laws. This time Rab and his gang had been caught violating one of the lesser laws.

Rab roused himself from sleep long enough to ascertain that things had not changed. Sure enough, Isaac was still mumbling his prayers and Jonah was still cursing. Physical reality slowly intruded and Rab became aware of sharp pain in both of his shoulders. He tried to relieve the pressure by standing on his feet. He pulled up on the chains, his feet clumsily searching for their footing on the stone floor. They were "asleep" and sharp needle-like pains shot through the souls of his feet, but this sensation was a welcome diversion to the discomfort in his shoulders and arms. He shook himself awake and twisted his hands to relieve some of the pressure on his wrists. His arms had long since gone numb, but the sharp pain from the wrist bands was beginning to force its way through to his brain. He kept his movements to a minimum in order to not attract the attention of his two companions. He was not ready to deal with either of them just yet. To ignore the increasing pain, he forced himself to review the events that had led to this ridiculous situation.

Months ago, at the last feast, Rab had decided to rob one of the currency exchange booths on the Temple grounds set up during festival times. For years Rab had watched these lucrative businesses with envy. They seemed to be the ideal scam perfected through years of greed. Every person who came to the Temple during festival time had to pay a Temple tax, similar to an admission ticket. Long ago, some High Priest had decreed that the necessary Temple tax could only be paid by a certain type of coin. Of course, the priests were assigned the task of making and distributing the coins. To attend the festival a traveler had to exchange his currency for the Temple coins at one of the approved venders. These vendors were free to charge any exchange rate they wanted for the coins. The vendors kept part of the profits as did the priests who oversaw them. Undoubtedly some of the profit found its way into the Temple treasury, but Rab figured most of it found its way into the personal treasuries of the High Priest and his business associates.

Though Rab normally skirted the religious establishment, he had thought this business was something he ought to consider. After all he was no longer a young man and a "legitimate" business was becoming more appealing with each passing festival and brush with the law. He had planned to purchase a vendor's license, but a few discrete inquiries had revealed that they were reserved for a chosen few, mainly relatives or close friends of the current High Priest or one of his assistants.

He then had tried extortion, but soon found that the Temple police could be as cruel and harsh as the Romans. The religious leaders had no reservations about employing their services, especially if money was involved. Rab had only succeeded in making himself known to them.

His street-wizened cunning had finally given in to his frustration and Rab had decided to just rob one of the vendors. The plan was simple. In the middle of the afternoon when the coffers were full and the crowds were greatest, he and Jonah would close in, knock a vendor in the head, take his money bags and disappear into the crowd.

After studying the movements of the venders and police, he and Jonah had made a couple of practice runs. But Rab had determined they needed someone to keep an eye out for any sudden changes in the routines of either the priests or the Temple police. That's why he had recruited Isaac, the most unlikely of men.

Chapter Three

Isaac had finally fallen asleep. Jonah was relieved and even quit his complaining.

"I didn't think that old man would ever shut up," Jonah remarked to Rab when he heard his leader's chains moving as Rab adjusted his stance. "Have you found out what happened?"

"Not yet, but I will. If he messed up, he will pay." Jonah didn't need any light to know the look of contempt that was on Rab's face. He had seen it often enough.

Isaac's sleep was fitful. He had tried to stay awake because he did not want to dream. Isaac hated the dark. More accurately he feared the dark. Even as an adult he rarely allowed himself to be caught in a place without light. But as much as he feared the dark, he dreaded falling asleep and even more the reoccurring nightmare that inevitably followed. This experience was proving to be the worst of his life, alternating between being in pitch black listening to Jonah's cursing and being in the terror of his dreams.

In recent years Isaac had tried to reach back into the depths of his memory to recall anything that had happened in his childhood to terrify him. There had to be some reason for his fear. At other times he consoled himself in his prayers. He believed for some reason that his fear of the dark and his unshakable confidence that God existed were related, but he was not sure how. It may have been the dream.

Like most dreams, Isaac's did not make much sense, but it was consistent. It always began in darkness. There were animals all around, sheep. He could hear them, smell them or maybe just sense them. There was a fire with men sitting around it talking and laughing. Isaac's father was there too. It was a peaceful, very pleasurable scene and Isaac always wished he could stay in that moment. But suddenly one of the men's heads jerked upward toward the night sky. The others looked in the direction he pointed and then everything changed. Suddenly everyone was moving around chaotically, frightened. Isaac's dream world exploded into brilliant light, not starlight or sunlight, but light emanating from strange beings in the sky. For some reason, Isaac could not move. There was more to the dream, Isaac knew, but it was at this point he always woke up, shaking with fright.

This time was no exception. His dream terror was again replaced by his fear of the dark. Even though it was not necessary, he closed his eyes again, hoping he could drift back to sleep, this time without the dream.

Unlike Rab and Jonah, Isaac was not accustomed to being in jail. In fact, he had never been in jail before. It is not that he had never contemplated criminal activity. In many ways for most of Isaac's life his heart had been as dark and evil as either that of Rab or Jonah. He had just never had the opportunity before. For thirty-eight of his forty years he had been an invalid, the victim of an unknown childhood malady. For all but the last few months of his life he had been totally at the mercy of others. His parents had borne that responsibility without complaint, but as Isaac grew, the more aware he had become of his limitations.

Despite all that a loving family could do, he increasingly saw himself as a victim. The older he became, the more despondent he grew. When his parents died, he all but gave up on life. No one in his home town of Bethlehem knew what to do for him. Finally the local priest arranged for him to be taken to Jerusalem where he could beg for food. For the last dozen or so years, he had lived near the Pool of Bethesda in north Jerusalem.

The Pool of Bethesda was the gathering place for every kind of the society's outcast: the crippled, lame and the sick. Most were attracted to the pool by the legend. As the legend went, from time to time an angel from God would come down and stir the water. The first person into the pool after the water was stirred would be healed. The priest, depositing him there, told him the story. Isaac did not know if it was true or simply a way for the priest to deal with his own guilt for abandoning him there. But suddenly one day, the waters actually moved with no visible sign of disturbance. Isaac's spirits soared at the prospect of being healed, but before he could even move toward the water, someone on the far side made it in. Isaac was amazed at the immediate response. The man came out rejoicing, evidently healed. For the next several months, Isaac asked for passers-by to position him first at one place and then another, always near the pool. But each time the water was stirred, someone else got in ahead of him. Isaac noticed that the ones who got in were either able to walk or they had someone to help them. Isaac had neither.

Actually he did have one man who seemed to care about him. Why, he did not know. Possibly it was simply because they were from the same hometown. This man from his past had happened to spot him one day as he begged beside the pool. Isaac could not help notice that Joshua, as he had called himself at that time, seemed to have no steady job. But he would come by the pool from time to time. Their conversations ranged in topic from their childhood lives in Bethlehem to current political conditions. Isaac often wondered if Joshua was using him as a guinea pig to practice his social skills, which were obviously lacking.

More likely, he had concluded, *he helps me out to assuage his conscience.*

Isaac did not know why, nor did he care. He was just glad to receive the silver coins Joshua tossed his way from time to time. A single one of them purchased enough bread to eat for almost a month. Unfortunately Joshua was never around when the waters were stirred, but apart from that, he had been a good friend right up until the day Isaac had been healed.

Chapter Four

"Isaac! Isaac! Wake up, Isaac, you're dreaming again," Rab rattled the arm shackle nearest to the sleeping old man.

Isaac roused himself, but before he could begin his memorized prayer, Rab's voice interrupted.

"Isaac! Isaac! I know you're awake so answer me, now!"

"Where are you? I can't see a thing. Dear God in heaven ..."

"Shut that stuff up, you cowardly ..."

"Leave it alone, Jonah, I'll handle this," Rab interjected. "Isaac, what happened back there? I thought we were clear."

"I don't know, Rab, I mean, Joshua, honest. I was right behind you guys. I'm a little older but I was keeping up step for step, when all of a sudden my legs ... they just gave out."

"What do you mean, gave out?" Rab asked with no compassion in his voice.

"I don't know. At first I thought I had tripped over something, but when I tried to get up my legs wouldn't move. It was just like they used to be, dead."

Isaac looked down at his legs. Though he could not see them in the darkness, he knew they had to be functioning on some level. Surely his arms could not be supporting his full weight. Isaac's legs had never filled out, but his arms, which he had depended entirely upon until he had been healed last year, were unusually strong.

But not that strong, he concluded, relieved that he was not completely paralyzed from the waist down again.

"Well, go on, tell us what happened," Rab interrupted Isaac's moment of silent relief.

"Like, I said, my legs stopped working, so I tried to drag myself behind one of the merchant's tables, but before I could get out of sight, the Temple police grabbed me," Isaac explained.

"You told them, didn't you? Jonah interrupted with a sneer. "I told you he was trouble, Rab. Right from the start I told you we didn't need him."

"I told you I would handle this, Jonah."

Jonah could feel Rab's hot breath on his face and it caused him to look away. Even though he could not see them, he knew Rab's coal black eyes were ablaze with anger. He dared not continue his accusations, and for a moment all was quiet in the darkness.

"Alright Isaac, what happened then?" Rab's voice was quieter now.

"They took me back to the temple to see if any of the merchants could identify me. None of them could and I thought I was going to be set free, when a group of priests came out. They must have noticed the commotion and asked what was happening. The merchants explained about the robbery, and one of the priests said he thought he knew who the thieves were." The words were pouring out of Isaac as rapidly as his prayers had been earlier.

"He went on to describe you two as petty thieves who were always hanging around the Temple during feast times. He knew of your attempted extortions and your trying to get a booth license. He said that your names and descriptions had been circulated among the Temple police. They had been waiting for you, Joshua," Isaac concluded.

"You're lying, old man. You're just trying to save yourself." Jonah could not control himself. "You told them where to find us. I know you did."

"I did not," Isaac protested. "They already knew. They even knew your escape route through the underground tunnels."

"How could they have known that?" Rab asked.

"I don't know, but I didn't tell them, I swear," Isaac responded. "Joshua, I wouldn't do that to you. If it hadn't been for you, I'd probably be dead by now. You've got to believe me, I didn't tell them anything."

The next few moments passed with only the sounds of Jonah's deep breathing from one side of the cell and Isaac's sobs from the other. In the middle, Rab was lost in thought.

Why did I ever ask Isaac to help us with the robbery? Sure, we needed some help, but there were plenty of men to choose from. Why Isaac?

Of course, Jonah had asked him the same question a hundred times. He had even protested the decision, but from the moment it was determined they needed help, Isaac had been Rab's only choice. *Why?*

Rab knew there were two possible answers, and they both involved the same strange issue- Isaac's mysticism-his belief in God. Not long after they had met at the pool, Isaac told Rab about his nightmares. At first Rab had thought he was just crazy, but finally decided there might be some substance to Isaac's nightly visions of heavenly beings. On one hand he desperately wanted to prove Isaac wrong. He would say, "There is no God, you stupid old man." But, on the other hand, Isaac's railings had been like flint against the cold steel of his heart. They produced sparks of light in the deep darkness. None had caught hold, but something akin to hope flickered every time Rab was with Isaac. And so whenever he was feeling especially morbid, Rab would drop by the pool.

But that all ended a year ago, Rab suddenly became aware of where his thoughts had taken him. The same place they always ended: at the time he went to the Pool of Bethesda to see Isaac, but Isaac was nowhere to be found.

"Isaac," Rab spoke as softly to him as his crude manner allowed. "I believe you. Calm down."

"Joshua, you've got to believe me. I wouldn't turn you in," Isaac continued.

"I said I believe you, now calm down," Rab said a

second time, but with little success in consoling his frightened friend. "Look, Isaac, why don't you tell me again how you got healed."

"Huh?" Isaac asked through muffled sobs.

"Tell me again how you got healed," Rab repeated quietly.

"Oh, come on, Rab. We've heard that stupid story a hundred times," Jonah could keep quiet no longer.

"I told you to shut up, Jonah," Rab interrupted. "Go on, Isaac. Tell me again."

"Again?" Isaac asked as he strained to wipe his cheeks with his shoulders. "Ok! Well, you know I was at the pool as always. One day this man came by and asked me if I wanted to get well. I told him I did but I didn't have anybody to help me when the water was stirred and somebody else always beat me into the water. He then said, 'Get up! Pick up your mat and walk.' At first I thought He was joking or something, but when I looked in His eyes I realized He was serious. At that moment, for some reason I believed He knew what He was doing and that I could actually walk."

"So what did you do old man?" Jonah jeered, acting as if he had not heard this before.

"Stay out of this, Jonah," Rab interrupted. "Go on Isaac."

"I just got up, like I had been doing it all of my life. It was amazing."

"What happened then," Rab asked, hoping to keep Isaac's mind occupied for a while longer.

"I rolled up my mat and left the pool area."

"Where were you going to go?" interrupted Jonah. "You didn't have any home."

"I don't know, I was just glad to be walking," Isaac said, ignoring the intended jab. "But I didn't get very far. I ran into some priests. They chewed me out for carrying my mat on the Sabbath."

"Those hypocrites!" volunteered Jonah.

Ignoring him, Isaac continued with his story, "I told them that the man who made me well told me to pick up my mat and walk. Then they asked who the man was. I told them that I had no idea who He was. I had never seen Him before, and He had disappeared into the crowd without introducing Himself."

Rab was glad that Isaac's relating of his story gave them all some relief from both Isaac's chanting and Jonah's ranting. But even as he asked his next question he realized Isaac's answer would destroy that peace.

"Who was he?"

Isaac hesitated because he knew his answer would reap insults. "I think He is God's Messiah," Isaac finally said.

"You're crazy, old man. That stuff is just legend," Jonah shot out.

Ignoring Jonah, Rab asked, Why do you think that, Isaac?"

Isaac, also ignoring Jonah responded, "Well, when I found out it was the Sabbath I decided to go up to the Temple and thank God personally for my healing. While I was in the Temple, that same man came up to me and said, 'See, you are well again. Stop sinning or something worse may happen to you.' The men with Him said He was Jesus. Since that time I have heard a lot about Him. Some call Him a teacher of the law; others call Him a prophet. Some believe, like I do, that He is actually the Messiah, the Son of God."

"I don't believe any of that garbage," Jonah interrupted again. "Neither do you, right Rab?"

Rab was silent. He wanted to agree with Jonah, but he didn't want to break the calm so he just decided to ignore Jonah's question.

"What else do they say about this man?" Rab asked Isaac.

"They say He has done many miracles, healed many

people, and that He even has the power to cast devils out of people. They also say that His teaching is with great power and authority."

"If He is a teacher of the law, why did He tell you to break the Sabbath law?" Jonah asked.

Rab and Isaac were surprised by Jonah's question and neither was sure how serious he was, but regardless of Jonah's motivation, it was a good question. Both pondered it in silence.

After a while Isaac attempted an answer, "I don't know, but I can tell you this, the religious leaders hate the man. It didn't take me long to find out that as far as they are concerned, He is a rebel. He doesn't play by their rules and He doesn't honor the way they abuse their positions."

"I heard one of them say that He is an imposter because He came from Galilee and everyone knows the true Messiah will be born in Bethlehem," Isaac added this last bit of information because he knew that all boys who were born in his hometown, even Joshua and Jonah, were taught this prophecy regarding the Messiah.

"I don't think there is such a person as the Messiah," Jonah said again.

This time Rab did not remain silent. "Jonah, it's that kind of thinking that is keeping you out of the Zealots. You are not aware of this, but one of the central beliefs of the Zealots is that God will one day send a man to free our homeland from foreign oppressors. He will be a descendant of King David and will re-establish the throne of His ancestor, David," Rab explained.

Neither Isaac nor Jonah had ever heard Rab say anything remotely positive on the subject of God, and an awkward silence settled like a blanket over the darkened cell. Realizing the impact his words had, Rab was somewhat embarrassed to have revealed so much of his inner hopes, and so he began cursing the pain in his shoulders. Sensing his diversion was not working, after a while he too became quiet.

"Well, I believe this man, Jesus, is the Messiah," Isaac finally said, breaking the silence. "I don't care what the priests say. Anyway I think they are just jealous of His popularity. They just want to hold on to their power over the people."

There was no response from either Rab or Jonah, and so after a moment, Isaac offered his final argument.

"If He is not the Messiah, how can He do the miracles He does? How did He heal me?"

Again, there was no response. Isaac really did not expect one, nor at that moment did he care. He had begun to realize that the tiny seed of faith which had been planted in his heart many years ago had just received some long needed nourishment. He quietly began to pray, not because of the darkness in his cell, but because of the light, dim as it was, in his soul.

Rab too sensed a change deep within. Despite everything, he found himself trying to understand the words of Isaac's prayer. As he fell back into a fitful sleep, Rab wondered if he would ever encounter this other Jesus, the one called the Messiah. If He was the true King of Israel what would this king think of him and his attempts to restore his kingdom?

Chapter Five

The quiet of the cell was suddenly shattered by the voices of angry men. In the next instant, the metal latches were released and golden yellow torchlight flooded the darkness as the huge wooden door was pushed open. The light illuminated the stone walls behind the prisoners. Aroused from sleep, Isaac and Jonah curiously watched shadows of three men now showing clearly on the nearby stone wall they were facing. It took a few moments before they realized the silhouettes, dancing with the approaching torches, belonged to themselves.

For some unexplained reason, Rab had been faced in the opposite direction, toward the hallway. He suddenly found the torches glaring in his face. He jerked his head sideways and squinted his eyes until they adjusted to the light. In addition to the men with torches, evidently another man was being brought into the small underground prison. Rab observed all that was taking place right before his eyes. Something was not right, but he could not clear his head enough to discern what it was. Even to a man who had seen the inside of more than one jail, the scene unfolding before him was bizarre.

Rab watched as the guards shoved the new prisoner through the door. Either the man tripped on the door jam or he had been tripped, for he fell headlong onto the stone floor right in front of Rab. Even the hardened murderer gasped as he looked more closely at the man fallen at his feet. Rab realized that the man's robe, which appeared dark red in the torchlight was actually completely soaked with blood, dried blood.

It was difficult to take his eyes off of the new prisoner, but for the briefest of moments Rab turned his attention to the guards. There were three of them. Two carried torches and the other was handling the prisoner. One of the guards then placed his torch in a holder on the wall and came to the assistance of the guard with the prisoner.

"Should we put him down in the hole?"

"Yeah, let's do. That's just what he deserves."

They shoved the man who stumbled passed Rab and toward a large stone lying on the floor near the wall. The prisoner tripped on the stone and fell onto his knees just beyond it.

"Move out of the way," the guard commanded, as he shoved the prisoner over with his foot then turned his attention to moving the stone. There was a large metal ring attached to the center of the stone and through it was a short rope. The guard grabbed the rope and pulled on it. He pulled again, but the stone barely moved.

"Help me with this," he said. "This thing is heavy. You push and I'll pull."

Checking to see that the prisoner was secure, the second guard added his weight and the two were able to scrape the stone across the floor. In the torchlight Rab could now see an opening in the floor, just barely large enough for a man to fit through. Being careful not to burn himself, the guard with the torch squatted down and pushed it partway into the opening revealing a small room below the cellar.

"Yeah, that's where he belongs while we continue our deliberation," said the guard with the torch. "It is nice and cozy down there."

The guard then shifted the torch so he could get a better look at the prisoner who was, with obvious difficulty, just then pushing himself up onto his knees. Another kick from the second guard and he went back down on his side.

"It's no use," said the guard with the torch. "We could drop him into the hole, but how would we get him out? Maybe we better just chain him up like the rest of these vermin."

Shrugging their shoulders the other two bent down,

grabbed the new prisoner by the shoulders and stood him on his feet. They shoved him back in the direction from which they came and stopped him right in front of Rab.

Rab watched all of this with increasing interest. He felt that something was not quite right about these guards, but his pain-fogged mind could not quite figure it out. Like one spying out a weakness or oversight in a potential adversary, the chained prisoner studied, as best he could, the three men as they went about their business. He felt sure these were not the regular guards. Neither were they Temple soldiers or even Roman soldiers.

Who are these men? Rab asked himself.

Looking more closely now, Rab spied a peculiar pattern in the fringe of one man's robe. As the guard bent down to shackle the new prisoner's foot, it had protruded out beyond the outer garment, which was just a common tunic. Rab had seen that design before; but where?

Rab struggled to remember where. Finally, he recalled. It was at the Temple.

These men are priests, Rab suddenly concluded. But that realization only generated more questions.

What are priests doing here? And in the middle of the night? Rab wondered. *Where are the regular guards? Why aren't they handling this prisoner?*

It was then that Rab noticed another man standing in the opened doorway, observing the proceedings. This man was dressed in the most ornate robe Rab had ever seen. Even in the darkened room the gold adornments of the purple ceremonial robe glistened in the torchlight. Before Rab could formulate a mental question concerning this man, he noticed that he wore a jeweled breastplate of some kind.

Is that the Ephod, the breastplate worn by the High Priest? Rab knew the answer before the words formed in his mind. Every petty thief within traveling distance of Jerusalem had dreamed of getting his hands on the High Priest's Ephod.

It was a one-of-a-kind piece of jewelry made of gold with twelve different jewels, one for each of the original twelve tribes of Israel. The Ephod was the equivalent of a king's crown jewels. The materials themselves were valuable enough, but there were several he knew who would pay plenty for the privilege of possessing it. Even from a distance Rab was awestruck by it. It was more spectacular, even in the poor light, than any description of it Rab had ever heard.

Rab's mind was alert now and racing. *What is the High Priest doing here?*

Then Rab remembered the obvious.

This is the High Priest's house, Rab reminded himself that this particular prison was built directly under the home of Caiaphas, the High Priest. Part of Caiaphas' official duties included passing judgment on certain classes of law breakers. Rab did not know whether it was for convenience or just because he liked the control, but Caiaphas had turned his cellar into a prison dungeon.

"What's going on?" Jonah whispered to Rab. He and Isaac had been straining to look over their shoulders, but without much success.

"It looks like Mister Caiaphas has just received another house guest for the night," Rab said through clenched lips hoping to not draw attention to himself.

The guards, or priests or whoever they were, had raised the new prisoner to his feet and were busy shackling him to the stone columns on the opposite side of the walkway directly across from Rab. They seemed to take no note of Rab or his companions.

Rab's attention was again drawn to the door. It appeared to him that there must have been a rather large number of men gathered upstairs. Whoever was there sounded as if they had just won some great battle. The noise of the celebration reminded Rab of some of the nights he had spent in the local taverns rejoicing with his comrades over a "victory for freedom" deed against the Romans or an unusually bountiful heist.

"I guess we'd better push that stone over the Hole, lest someone fall in there," the torch guard said.

The two went back over and pushed and pulled the stone lid over the opening.

When the "guards" completed their task of securing the Hole they again approached the new prisoner. They stepped up to the man, now hanging by his wrist shackles, and with a derisive laugh, one said, "You're not so powerful now are you, preacher man." And with that, each in turn spit in his face, the last one giving him a hard slap across his jaw. Then, almost as if by command they pivoted and marched toward the door.

Rab's eyes followed them as they filed out of the room. He was surprised that they failed to remove the torch from the wall or even to bolt the door.

"Incompetent fools!" Rab said audibly, but not loud enough to be heard by anyone, except his cell mates.

Rab watched as the weight of the heavy door pulled it open several inches. Through the opening Rab could still hear the clamorous proceedings upstairs. Though his curiosity about what was happening was great, his attention was soon drawn back to the man covered in blood who now hung by his wrists barely two arm's lengths in front of him.

Chapter Six

Rab began to inspect the new cell mate. He noticed first that he was a rather stout man, no stranger to hard labor. His hands, extended upward by the shackles, were covered with calluses. His forearms, now exposed by the fallen sleeves of his robe, were thick and muscular.

He is not a thief or professional man, Rab concluded. Then Rab recalled that one of the priests had called him a "preacher man." Rab was thinking that this man did not look like a preacher, but then decided he did not know any preachers, only priests. A few years back there had been a preacher by the name of John.

Rab tried to recall what he had heard of John. John had lived in the desert, refusing to come to the city. Many had gone out to hear him including some of Rab's friends. Several of these had come back having made resolutions to go straight. A few of them, Rab remembered, had actually succeeded in giving up their shady practices. One close associate had dropped out of the Zealots and had gone back home to help his father on the family farm. He had spoken of being dunked into the Jordan River as a symbol of his becoming religious, as Rab called it. Rab had simply written him off as a weak-willed man who could be manipulated by any man with smooth words, working his own angle or scheme.

But Rab also recalled that that preacher, John the Baptizer, had had his head served on a platter at a banquet given by King Herod. He had decided then that maybe the preacher wasn't all bad. If he could incur the wrath of that tyrant, Herod, he must have done something right. Now before him was another preacher who had incurred the wrath of the powers that be.

What in the world could he have done to have his robe completely covered with blood? Rab asked himself.

He doesn't show signs of being beaten, at least not that much, Rab noted. *Maybe he is a murderer. But I have killed people and I never got that bloody*, Rab continued debating himself.

Finally he tore his gaze away from the robe and looked at the man's face. Rab was somewhat startled to discover the man was not unconscious as he had assumed, but instead was looking directly back at him. Their eyes met.

Immediately Rab was locked in a contest of wills. Who would look away first? In the animal-like circles he ran, any sign of weakness would be noted for future exploitation. Sometimes it was action that counted, a fist or knife. At other times it was a contest of words. You didn't have to be right; you just had to be the loudest or hold your ground the longest. Often though, it was simply a matter of who could stare down his adversary. The one who held his gaze the longest gained an added measure of advantage over his opponent.

Rab was no stranger to these contests. His very life had depended on being strong. As a result, he had stared into the eyes of some of the meanest men on the face of the earth. Looking into those eyes, Rab had seen such despair that it sometimes made his skin crawl. He had seen darkness in the eyes of men so deep it was like looking into Death itself. And on at least one occasion, he had seen such pure evil he knew he was looking not into the soul of a man but into the eyes of a demon, if not the devil himself. It had made him want to vomit, but he had never looked away, not once.

As Rab began the contest, he braced himself for the same kind of malevolence. This had to be one bad man. But what he met instead was something totally unexpected. The eyes of this man were soft and gentle. Rab was surprised; no, stunned! Holding his glare, Rab tried to recall something in his experience that connected with the message that was communicated to him in this man's eyes.

What is this? What is this guy trying to do? This could

not be ... love? Rab knew absolutely nothing about love, but he did know that this was not the wicked, perverted love of a man lusting for another. Rab had seen that look as well. This was a look of interest – no, concern, for him. The fellow prisoner's eyes communicated somehow to Rab that though he himself was in pain and deep trouble, he was more concerned about Rab and his trouble or pain.

What was worse, this man seemed to look deeply into Rab's soul. Rab immediately wanted to find a way to hide what was inside. Though they had never seen one another before, it seemed as if this new prisoner knew everything there was to know about him, all of his wicked deeds and thoughts, even his doubt and pain. Yet his gaze communicated love and acceptance. There was even sorrow, not pity. Rab somehow knew the man was feeling what Rab had experienced. He seemed to know that Rab had been greatly damaged and that his life had not gone according to a proper plan. Rab was suddenly vulnerable and he did not like it.

Without warning the thief began to think of the father he had never known. Without breaking his gaze, Rab wondered, *Why am I thinking about my father?* This man was roughly his own age yet, his eyes seemed more like those of a father, like those of the white haired men who went to Temple each day for prayers. They often smiled at him as they passed and greeted him with, "Shalom!" But it was the peace and love in their eyes that, despite his hard exterior, always touched something deep within him. He had fought against that feeling as well. They made him wish he had known his Father and Grandfather, but he couldn't afford such childish emotions. The man across from him was now making him feel the same way.

Rab found feelings rising within him he could not even identify. The dam he had built around his heart was beginning to crack. The contest was forgotten. Rab wanted to look away, needed to look away; but he could not. His eyes were transfixed on those of the man covered in blood.

"Hey, what's going on?" Jonah broke the silence.

"I don't know," Isaac answered. "But they must have left a torch in here. We can see. Hallelujah!"

"Keep your voice down," Rab barked the order just above a whisper, glad for the diversion. "They also left the door open. If they hear you they will come back and take the torch out."

"Who's the new guy?" Jonah asked, his back to the new prisoner.

"I don't know," Rab began cautiously. "We haven't been formally introduced."

Isaac and Jonah were waiting for Rab to make the first move. They were respectful of his position as leader and they waited for him to establish his authority with the new prisoner. Rab was still trying to regain his composure. After a few minutes he spoke.

"My name's Bar-Abbas, but most call me Rab," Rab spoke quietly and as evenly as possible. Nodding his head in the direction of each man, he continued, "That's Isaac and this is Jonah." As Rab mentioned each man's name, Isaac raised one of his shackled hands in a gesture of greeting, but Jonah only grunted.

Up to this point the man had not taken his eyes from Rab, but though obviously weak and in pain, he nodded toward Jonah and then smiled when Isaac's name was called and then looked his way.

"Hello, Isaac. I haven't seen you in over a year. How are your legs?" the man asked.

Startled, Isaac jerked his head as far as he could toward the man's voice, but could not see him.

"Who are you? Do I know you?" Isaac asked, now trying to rotate in his shackles. "How do you know about my legs?"

"Have they remained strong or have you had trouble with them?" the man asked, ignoring Isaac's questions.

Isaac was not sure what to say. Natural defenses built by years of pain usually stopped him from telling much about himself, but the tone in this man's voice, and his obvious familiarity with him, were brushing them aside.

"I was doing really good until," Isaac hesitated. "Until I got involved with these guys in a ..."

"Shut up, Isaac," Jonah interrupted. "You don't even know who this guy is. He could have been put in here by those goons out there to get evidence on us."

Ignoring the interruption, the man continued his conversation with Isaac. "Isaac, do you recall I told you to stop sinning or something worse might happen to you?"

There was a moment of silence, then...

"Master! Is that you? Of course it's you. I recognize your voice now." Isaac responded excitedly. Suddenly his voice dropped off. After a moment he continued, "Is that what happened to my legs at the Temple? I'm sorry, Lord. I should have paid attention to your warning. I had no business being part of a robbery. I did good for a long time, but my friend here, Joshua, needed help and I needed the money. Jobs are hard to get with no training you know. And anyway, like Joshua said, those so-called priests at the Temple are robbing people and ..."

"Isaac," the new prisoner's voice had a firmness.

Isaac fell silent. After a moment he began to weep. "Master, will you forgive me?" Isaac's words began gushing out of him as if they had been pent up and under pressure. "All my life I have been bitter and angry. Deep inside I have been hateful and resentful, to everyone and everything. I wasn't even thankful for the good things that came my way. I always wanted more. The robbery was just my way of trying to get some pay back. I'm sorry. Please forgive me, Jesus. Please forgive me. When I get out of this prison, I am going to Temple and make my sacrifices for my sin. I promise." Isaac continued to sob.

When he had quieted down somewhat Jesus said, "Isaac, it is written, 'The sacrifices of God are a broken spirit; a broken and contrite heart.'" Then Jesus added in a soft but assertive voice, "You are forgiven, Isaac. Be at peace."

"That's just great, you stupid old man," Jonah retorted. "You just signed our death warrant."

Isaac paid no attention to Jonah, but instead, slipped into one of his prayers.

"I told you both to keep your voices down," Rab, who had been watching this exchange in unbelief, suddenly hissed. Both men became quiet, and so Rab turned to look once again at the man across from him, being careful this time to avoid his eyes. He directed his questions to Isaac.

"Isaac, is this the man who healed you at the Pool of Bethesda?"

Isaac did not respond.

"Isaac," Rab said again, this time with more authority. "Is this the man who healed you?"

"Yes," Isaac said simply.

"You are sure?"

"Yes, I recognize his voice and he did warn me about sinning again. I didn't tell anybody about that."

Rab pondered these things before speaking again. "So you're telling us that this man is Jesus, the Messiah?"

In spite of the lightness growing in his heart, Isaac answered Rab's questions calmly.

"Yes," he said.

"What else do you know about Him?" Rab continued.

"All I know is what people said about Him. He was healing people and teaching. Some said He cast demons out of people. I don't know. He sure helped a lot of people," Isaac said.

"Is that it?" Rab probed.

"I guess He made a lot of people angry, too," Isaac offered. "I wasn't there but I heard that a few days ago He went into the Temple, turned over the tables of the money changers and other merchants, then ran them all out with a whip. They didn't like that. But, like I said, I think the religious ones, the priests were just jealous of His popularity."

Rab looked once more at the man across from him. He was about to ask Him to confirm Isaac's description when Jonah interrupted. He directed his question to the man behind his back.

"Alright, Mister, all three of us here were born in Bethlehem. You can tell we ain't scholars, but we do know this so called Messiah is supposed to be born in our home town. Right, Isaac?" He didn't wait for Isaac to answer.

"Bethlehem isn't that big a place so I figure if you really are from Bethlehem, one of us here, Rab or Isaac or me, would know you." Jonah was surprised no one had cut him off, and so he continued.

"So tell us about your birth," he challenged and then added sarcastically, "I'm sure you don't remember it but your Mom and Dad surely filled you in about it."

Jesus waited a moment or two and then responded to Jonah's questions. "I was born in Bethlehem. My Mother's name is Mary. She is of the tribe of Judah. My Step-Father is Joseph, a carpenter, also of the tribe of Judah. They lived in Galilee but had come to Bethlehem at the orders of Augustus Caesar to register for tax purposes. My actual Father is the God of Abraham, Isaac and Jacob."

Jonah started to interrupt at this statement but was cut off as Jesus continued.

"My birth was announced in the sky by a brilliant star. It was also proclaimed to a group of local shepherds by a host of angels rejoicing because of the peace I would bring to the world."

If his shackles had not been made of forged steel,

Isaac would surely have torn them from their fastenings at this last revelation.

"Jesus, what did you say? Did you say angels? Were they clothed in brightly colored robes and did they sing and ...?" Isaac could not get the words out fast enough.

"Yes, Isaac," Jesus replied. "You were with your Father on the hillside outside Bethlehem. You saw the angels. You were brought as a boy to the cave in which I was born. It was a gift to you from my Heavenly Father designed to help you bear the difficulties of your life. Sadly though, your bitterness over your physical difficulties allowed the enemy to block out some of your memory and you were left in your fear. You are freed now from your fear and, Isaac, know this: the Father still has a plan for you. You will inspire more in your death than most do in their lives."

With this Isaac turned his face toward the wall and began to weep. But unlike so many times in the past, these were tears of joy. He was finally at peace. "I knew I wasn't crazy ... "

Jonah spoke up, "Wait a minute, what about my other question. If you are from Bethlehem, how come none of us know you?"

"Jonah, my family lived in Bethlehem only a short time. My Step-Father was warned by an angel from God that my life was in danger and so he escaped with my Mother and me to Egypt. When we returned, my parents were directed by Father God to settle back in Galilee. I grew up in Nazareth. All of this was done to accomplish God's plan. It is recorded in The Book.

What started as fascination for Rab as he listened to these amazing claims was now turning into a growing sense of agitation. He was not sure why, but something about this man's story made him suspect that this man, although they had never met before tonight, had already impacted his own life as well. Rab did not know how. He could not even put his finger on why he thought so.

"Bring him upstairs and tie him to the chair!" The order was shouted loud enough that even the prisoners in the cellar were jarred by its ferocity. An instant later four disguised priests burst through the door and went directly to the new prisoner, Jesus. The first man hit Jesus sharply across the face with the back of his hand. While one held a torch, two unshackled Jesus' feet and then His hands. The fourth propped Him up as He sagged toward the ground, His legs unable to fully support His weight. They half carried, half dragged Jesus out the door and up the stone stairway. As soon as it was quiet again Isaac spoke up.

"What happened? What did they do with Jesus?"

"Shhh! Be quiet! They left the door open again. They might hear us," Rab commanded.

"What did they do with Jesus?" Isaac asked again, softly but persistently.

"I don't know. If you will keep quiet, maybe we can hear something," Rab scowled in Isaac's direction.

Chapter Seven

For the next hour or so, the three prisoners listened intently to the gathering of men upstairs. For the most part, they listened in silence, but from time to time Isaac or Jonah had to make a comment or ask a question.

"Rab, can you tell what's going on?" Isaac asked.

"It sounds like a trial," Rab commented at one point.

"How can that be? Isn't it against the law to have a trial at night?" Jonah asked.

"You have learned some things, haven't you?" Rab answered. "Yes it is."

"Then if it is a trial, it is illegal," Isaac said.

"You got it."

"Then why are they doing it?" Isaac asked.

"It sounds like they want this guy so bad, they are willing to bend the rules to get it done," Jonah surmised.

"What's taking so long?"

"If you guys will be quiet maybe I can find out," Rab snarled.

More time went by as the voices from upstairs increased in volume and in hostility. Several angry outbursts occurred. Each one followed by the pleas of someone or another to calm down. But little calm prevailed. It sounded more like a pack of wild wolves tearing at a downed lamb than a court of law.

"What is all the hollering about? What are they saying?"

"They seem to be having trouble finding enough evidence to convict Him," Rab replied.

"Convict Him of what? What could He have done ..."

Isaac's question was interrupted by a loud cheer from outside. Then an ominous hush settled over the whole building.

"I think they are coming back," Rab broke the silence.

The door burst open. Rab tried to act disinterested as he watched the same four men drag Jesus into the room. Two held Him up while a third again shackled His hands and feet to the columns. They left without a word or even a glance toward the other prisoners. Rab studied Jesus in the eerie torchlight. He noticed that now Jesus was unable to stand at all. His face was bruised and bleeding from several new cuts. Both eyes were beginning to swell shut and His hair was matted with blood.

"Man! You look terrible," Rab said more as an observation than in sympathy. "I don't know what you did, but they sure don't like you."

"Jesus," Isaac asked turning his head but unable to see. "Are you alright? What did they do to you?"

In spite of His condition, Jesus smiled in Isaac's general direction and said, "It's OK, Isaac. I can handle it. My Father has promised me His strength. It's part of His plan."

"Part of your Father's plan?" Jonah spoke up. "What kind of Father puts his Son through something like this? I thought my old man was bad; yours must hate your guts," he said, and then concluded with, "and you must be crazy to go along with any stupid plan like that."

For a moment there was only the sound of Jesus' heavy breathing, but when He had gotten His breath, He finally spoke.

"I know all of this seems foolish to you," Jesus replied slowly, occasionally wincing from the pain of His split lips. "Actually, there is great wisdom and love behind the plan. As far as my going along with it, my Father gave me a choice. I knew what was before me and so it was a difficult choice. But when I was confident that no other way was available to satisfy Father God's justice and to defeat the enemy, I chose to look beyond the sorrow and suffering to the joy my death will bring."

Rab had been trying to absorb all that was going on

and being said. He really had no reference point to understand any of it. Finally he blurted out, "You don't make any sense. You are the guy who healed Isaac. He thinks you're the promised Messiah. First you tell this story about being born in Bethlehem with angels and all. And now you're saying you're suffering because your Father wants you to. You believe you're going to die to satisfy God's justice or something and that will bring joy."

Uncharacteristically, Rab continued to air his confusion out loud. "And who is this enemy you're going to defeat by dying? How do you defeat someone by dying?"

Jonah agreed, "Yeah! I always figured the best way to defeat an enemy was for him to do the dying!"

"Why don't you guys just shut up and leave Him alone. I'm sure He doesn't feel like answering all of your stupid questions," Isaac protested in uncharacteristic boldness.

"Well now, who appointed you this man's protector?" Jonah snapped back. "Isaac, if you understand what He is saying, why don't you explain it to us."

Isaac was angered by Jonah's attack, but he did not know how to respond.

Taking as deep a breath as possible with His bruised ribs, Jesus let out a sigh and responded to Isaac. "Thanks, Isaac, for your concern, but I am holding up, and I welcome your questions, all of them. Jonah, the religious leaders have reminded me many times that the Messiah does not come from Galilee, but not once have they stopped to ask where I was born. You are the first person here in Jerusalem to ask me that. I hope it expresses a heart seeking to know truth."

"Truth! Huh! What do you know of truth? Despite what Isaac says - who, by the way, if you haven't noticed happens to be a little crazy - my hunch is that you're no messiah, but just a common criminal," Jonah retorted with rancor, unusual even for him. "Besides, if you are supposed to be the Deliverer of Israel, why don't you deliver yourself out of this prison. If you can do that, all three of us will follow you. Right, Rab?" Jonah said as he strained to catch his leader's eye. "At least as far as the door," he concluded with a derisive laugh.

Jonah fully expected Rab to enjoy his joke, and was surprised when Rab did not respond at all. Straining harder to see him, Jonah noticed that Rab was peering intently toward the man who was again hanging directly in front of him. He seemed to be studying this Jesus.

It was almost quiet in the cell, the stillness being broken only by the labored breathing of Jesus and an occasional cackle of laughter drifting through the door from upstairs. Jonah had stopped swearing. Even Isaac was still. But at least in the case of Rab, outward appearances were deceiving. His mind was racing, trying to sort out the clamor of thoughts and questions demanding his attention.

Nothing about this man made any sense and yet something He had said earlier made Rab believe that somehow their lives were entangled.

But what was it he said and how does it affect me?

Rab continued to study Jesus in the dim light. He could tell that He was in physical pain, sure, but beyond that Rab did not see a man distraught or even disturbed over the condition He was in or the treatment He was receiving. For a while Rab thought Jesus had fallen asleep, but then noticed that his lips were moving, though He was making no sound.

Is he talking to himself? Rab wondered. *No! He's praying*, Rab concluded.

Maybe he's crazy, like Isaac, only worse, Rab considered. *But if He is crazy, He has to be the craziest man I have ever met or heard of: to believe He is on a suicide mission to save mankind while He gets the life beat out of Him by those power-hungry priests.*

But Rab knew that the man across from him did not

have the demeanor of a lunatic. He was taking this much too calmly, unless of course He had completely lost touch with reality. Rab needed more information.

"Jesus," Rab began quietly seeking to appear interested but not soft, "you said you were born in Bethlehem, right?"

Jesus slowly looked up and looked directly into Rab's eyes. Again, Rab was taken aback and dropped his gaze slightly, but he pressed on. "It's kind of hard to tell in this light, so I'll just ask, 'How old are you anyway?'"

"I am almost exactly thirty-three and a half years old," Jesus replied summoning his strength to express interest. "Why do you ask?" Jesus was obviously interested in pursuing this conversation with Rab.

"Oh, I don't know, I was just trying to figure out whether or not our paths had crossed before," Rab replied as casually as he could and then added, "As Jonah said, I'm from Bethlehem, too."

Though he never considered himself a social being, he had never had trouble carrying on a simple conversation before, especially with other crooks. But he was struggling here. Then he remembered the thing that had bothered him earlier.

"Did you say your folks had to leave Bethlehem because you were in some kind of danger or something?"

'Yes, my Step-Father had been warned of the danger in a dream and we immediately fled to Egypt," Jesus said quietly.

"What kind of danger? Who would want to hurt a baby?" Even as the words were being formed in his mouth, a cold chill began to crawl through Rab's body. He knew the answer before he even asked the question. Looking at this strong, but gentle man across from him, for an instant he preferred not to hear the answer. This man, this Jesus, was the reason for all of the pain in his life. It was Jesus that King

Herod had tried to kill. His birth had caused Rab's parents, brothers and sisters to be murdered. It was He who had caused him to be an orphan, to live on the streets like an animal. Because of Jesus, all hope for a normal life had been stolen from him. Rab was a social outcast because of the man hanging directly in front of him. Rab knew he was a thief and a murderer and now he realized he was in this cell right now because – of the man directly across from him.

Rab looked once more into the eyes of the man, Jesus. It was as if he knew that this would be the last time he would look upon Him with any kind of favor. Even as Jesus began to confirm what he suspected, Rab felt that the pent up hatred in his heart was about to be unleashed.

"Yes, Joshua Bar-Abbas," Jesus began slowly. You are correct. I was the object of King Herod's fear and jealousy. When Herod was told of my birth by the kings from the East who came to pay me homage, he asked them to report back to him of my whereabouts. He told them he wanted to come and worship me even as they had. But my heavenly Father warned the kings in a dream of Herod's deceit and his true intention of murdering me. The Eastern kings returned home another way."

Rab became aware that his very personality seemed to be splitting in two. At once he was fascinated by the story he was hearing for it making sense of his tragic life. But at the same time the animal he had become was taking on a new focus of hostility. He felt as if he would explode. He was not sure how his outward appearance was remaining the same. In fact, he thought he could feel the darkness which had risen out of his spirit begin to constrict the muscles in his face. If Jesus was aware of the darkness taking over Rab's whole being, He did not let on, but continued his explanation.

"When Herod finally learned he had been outwitted by the eastern kings, he was furious. He gave orders to kill all boy babies in Bethlehem and the surrounding area," Jesus said holding His gaze upon Rab with what seemed to be an even greater sense of compassion. "Many innocent children died at his hands. Others, like yourself, Joshua, were hidden by their parents and orphaned by the brutal acts of the soldiers," Jesus said quietly and then added. "I am sorry, Joshua."

For what seemed to him like an eternity, Rab could not respond. But then he could hold his peace no longer. A lifetime of failure, sorrow and pain needed expression. He suddenly lurched forward ignoring both the stiffness in his muscles and the new cuts in his wrists created by the shackles which kept him just out of reach of the man across from him.

"Sorry? You're sorry?!" Rab exploded, completely forgetting his present state. "Well that certainly makes everything alright doesn't it. What do you expect me to do? Just say, 'Forget it! Everything's fine now.'?" The words exploded directly from his now unguarded heart like a volcano belching out years of pent up heat and pressure, fire and brimstone.

Jonah, who had shown little interest in the exchange up to this point, suddenly came alive. "That's it, Rab, you tell Him. I knew He was a phony, a fake. He ain't no messiah. He's just a liar, probably a thief too. Too bad Herod didn't kill Him. If we wasn't tied up I'd kill Him myself right here and now!" Jonah wasn't sure what this was about, but he knew he was on Rab's side.

Isaac had also been jarred from the inner peace he had been enjoying. He too was startled by Rab's sudden outburst. He had suspected that Rab had a very dark side but he had never seen him act anything like this. It was as if he had been taken over by a demon, or a hord of them. At first Isaac wondered how Jesus was taking all of this. Strain as he might, he could not turn far enough to see Him. But his concern, or curiosity, was interrupted by more shouts. But these were coming from outside.

Chapter Eight

"What's going on down here?" a priest suddenly burst into the room carrying a torch in one hand and a whip in the other. He had not taken time to put on his guard disguise.

In response Rab bellowed, "You better get this man out of my sight. I don't care if I am shackled to these posts, I'll find a way to kill Him right here in this jail."

Jonah was screaming in agreement. Isaac's prayers added to the chaos.

As several other priests poured into the room the first priest stopped directly between Rab and Jesus. He looked first in disgust at Rab and then at Jesus.

"What's the matter, preacher, some of your parishioners take offense at something you said?" he jeered as he pushed the handle of his whip sharply into Jesus' mid-section. By this time others had reached the prisoners. One had shoved his torch into Rab's face. The sudden heat caused Rab to cringe and the light caused him to jerk his head to one side and close his eyes again.

"What's the matter you rat," the priest all put spit the words in his face. "Don't like the light?"

"What's going on down here?"

The words were spoken with obvious authority, and the priests, turned jailors, reacted immediately to them.

"We are just having a little disturbance, sir," one of the priests said. "It looks like Bar-Abbas here has taken offense at 'the Messiah.' Nothing we can't handle."

Everything seemed to stop as the High Priest, Caiaphas himself, walked into the prison. The first priest quickly stepped aside as the High Priest stopped between the two prisoners. Caiaphas turned his back on Jesus and looked directly at Bar-Abbas. He could tell that his prisoner was still having difficulty controlling himself. Caiaphas did not know why, nor did he care.

"So this is the infamous Jesus Bar-Abbas, is it," began the High Priest as he looked in disgust at Rab. "You have made yourself a pest to my associates at the Temple: tempting my priests with bribes, stealing from the vendors. What do you plan next, taking the golden lampstand out of the Temple itself? Certainly you have little respect for the faith of your Fathers. But I am told that thievery is not the worst of your pursuits." He paused for effect. "I understand your specialty is dispatching Roman soldiers to their eternal reward."

The High Priest enjoyed the instant effect his words had on the prisoner, and though he could see only Rab's face he also noted the other two thieves' reactions as they stiffened against their restraints.

"Now what are we going to do with you and your cohorts in crime?" he pondered aloud as he studied Rab's face. He then slowly turned toward Jesus.

"Quite ironic don't you think," he mused. "We go for years with little business in this humble facility and tonight we have two revolutionaries; two men intent it seems on over-throwing the government."

Looking back and forth at the two prisoners, Caiaphas, who obviously enjoyed being the focus of attention regardless of whom it was from, continued, "We have two Jesuses – in fact, two would be saviors. One calls himself *Jesus, the Son of the Father,* and despite his lack of respect for the faith of his Fathers, he is bent on freeing us from the pagan Romans. The other calls Himself *Jesus, the Son of the Heavenly Father*. If we would believe Him, we would believe He is come to re-claim the throne of David and set up the Kingdom of God on earth."

The High Priest held his hands out toward the two men in a mock gesture of reconciliation. He spoke directly to the prisoners. "You two ought to be allies. After all you have the same goals." Pulling his hands back to his body and crossing them over the Ephod on his chest he concluded, "But it seems you are not getting along too well in this life. Maybe you will get along better in the next."

Then, as if he was suddenly extremely tired, the High Priest turned to the priest who was holding the whip. "Wake up the captain of my personal guard. I want these men prepared to be taken to Governor Pilate at first light."

"All of them?" the priest asked, somewhat confused by this development.

"Yes, all of them," Caiaphas snorted as he turned toward the door. "They are all rebels. I'm sure Pilate will be glad to know it is Jesus Bar-Abbas and his thugs who have been killing his soldiers. Who knows, he may even reward us. And as for the so-called "King of Kings" here, I think we have enough evidence to prove to Pilate that this other Jesus is also an enemy of Rome." His voice could still be heard as he ascended the stairs. "It's almost dawn. I have to clean up and change clothes. These are dirty and torn."

With little more than a scowl, one of the priests waved his whip before the two men facing him and said, "You boys better settle down now. You're going to need your strength. You have a big day ahead of you." With this he sneered and motioned the others out of the dungeon. This time they remembered to take the torch and lock the door.

Chapter Nine

The first rays of sunlight had not yet begun to spill over the Mount of Olives when the first of the four soldiers pushed open the large outer door of Caiaphas' cellar. The other three shoved Rab, Isaac and Jonah out onto the stone patio where they fell into a heap. In the midst of curses and prods from the blunt ends of spears, the three prisoners finally got some feeling back into their limbs, and began to make their way eastward down the small winding street that led in the general direction of the Temple. The first soldiers carried torches which aided them, but not those behind. The prisoners stumbled often, sometimes tripping on the uneven cobble stones, but more often just becoming tangled in the chains which shackled their ankles together.

Isaac and Jonah seemed totally absorbed in the task of just staying on their feet and thus avoiding the foul temper of the soldiers, who repeatedly showed their displeasure at having been roused from their beds at such an early hour. Rab's mind, on the other hand, wandered beyond the unpleasantries of the Temple soldiers. He began to picture in his mind the reception he would get when he was delivered over to the Romans as an insurrectionist and murderer of their comrades. He looked around, grateful that it was not quite light. He did not want his companions to see the anxious look that must surely be on his face. In a strange sort of way, he was grateful too for the sound of the chains as they slammed against the stones of the street.

Now that the three prisoners had gotten the hang of walking in step, the sound they made had become rhythmic, almost musical. Under different circumstances, the sound could have been almost pleasurable. Rab could barely make out the south western slope of Mount Moriah, their destination. Beyond that was the Mount of Olives, and beyond that, the road that led south to Bethlehem. The very first hint of a new day was beginning to push through the darkness in front of them, and the thought of never taking that road again, suddenly made Rab feel extremely sad. Each step took the little group further into the valley that lay just before the final ascent up Moriah, past the Temple and then on up to Fortress Antonia.

As the sunlight was attempting to search its way up and over the eastern slope of the Mount of Olives, the soldiers and their prisoners were traveling downward into the darkness of the valley. Rab's emotions were so jumbled he was glad each stuttering step took him further from the advancing light. Somehow it seemed appropriate, but all too soon the little shuffling group's descent into the valley ended and they turned northward to begin their ascent toward Fortress Antonia itself.

As the light from above began to find its way into the valley, Rab roused his mind into action. He decided to study the soldiers, to look for any sign of weakness he might exploit for escape. It was hopeful that there were only four of them. But try as he might he could not concentrate on the matter at hand. Maybe the beatings had taken more out of him than he had realized. The encounter with the High Priest himself had been almost terrifying, but the greatest effect had come simply by the look in the eyes of Jesus, the so-called 'Son of the Heavenly Father.'

What became of Him? Rab wondered. *I'm almost certain the High Priest gave orders for Him to be taken to Pilate along with us, but why did they not bring Him?*

Then he had an inspiration of sorts. *It's too bad I didn't think to offer to kill that guy myself. What a missed opportunity. That phony, Caiaphas, surely wanted Him dead. Those priests broke every rule in the book to convict Him. They probably could have gone one further and just let my little gang take care of their problem.*

Rab swore to himself as the next thought emerged.

They might have even paid us for it. It would sure beat turning him, and us, over to the Romans.

The last thought brought Rab back to reality. What lay ahead would not be pretty. The thief was all too aware that Herod had built the huge walled platform and named it Fortress Antonia. Among other purposes, it was where his soldiers were barracked. Surely that was their destination on this day, and with it being Feast time, no doubt Pilate himself would be in Jerusalem.

Rab's upper body suddenly shuddered. Without breaking the mournful stride, he quickly jerked the chain on his right wrist forward so he could pull his robe more tightly around his neck. Rab knew his body was reacting to more than the cool morning air, but he preferred no one else know. He looked up briefly to see if anyone had noticed. Isaac, who was shuffling along quite close to his back in an unsuccessful attempt to keep his distance from Jonah, was lost in his prayers. Evidently once Jonah realized the guards had little interest in the prisoners as long as they proceeded at a reasonable pace, the youngest in their group began a verbal barrage against the oldest. He had been quiet at first but was surprisingly loud now and punctuated his curses with occasional jerks on the wrist chain against the one he still felt responsible for their present condition. Rab wondered if Jonah really knew how bad their situation could become, especially with Pilate in town. Again, a shudder rumbled through his entire body.

If only I had had a chance to kill that... Rab cursed under his breath.

Rab doubted that Pontius Pilate, the Roman Procurator or Governor as he was also called, had ever heard of him. After all, the Governor spent most of his time in Ceasarea and only came to Jerusalem when necessity dictated it. Feast times were on that short list. But the Governor's reputation was well known, especially among Rab's companions, and their hatred for him had only grown since his appointment three years earlier.

At first, the Zealots assumed Pilate's initial harsh treatment of any Jew caught breaking the Roman laws was simply to establish his authority. But soon, it became obvious to even the most conciliatory citizen that Pontius Pilate hated the Jews and despised their customs. Most notably he considered their religious principles and laws contemptuous prejudices. Even Rab, who had no good thing to say for any Roman, could tell that, unlike his predecessors, the latest appointment from Rome treated the Jewish leaders as religious bigots, not to be worked with but to be scorned, ridiculed and held in check by force.

The procession was now about half way up the slope toward the Fortress and he noticed the city was beginning to come alive. Rab's mouth was extremely dry as he and his crew shuffled along. He knew that soon the white stone streets would be crowded. Even now the early light revealed small groups rousing themselves from various places of shelter they had found in the festival-swollen population of the capital city.

What a shame, Rab chided himself. *The crowd this year must be the largest ever. If only we hadn't got caught.*

Rab shook his head to clear his mind. He could not dwell on the past. He began to look around, to observe more carefully where they were. Though he hadn't gotten much sleep he knew if he ever wanted to sleep anywhere again, other than with his Fathers, he had to find a way to escape. Soon they would arrive at the Fortress. Rab assumed they would be taken along the west wall. Rab also knew, because he had walked it off on more than one occasion, that there remained only two hundred paces to the western or "business" entrance to the Fortress Antonia.

Rab was never much of a scholar, but he had always been fascinated by the Fortress of Antonia, as its builder

Herod the Great, had named it in honor of the famous Roman Caesar, Mark Anthony. It was part of Herod's massive construction project on top of Mt. Moriah or Mt. Zion as it was called, and it was a monstrous fort. Its walls were constructed of seven courses of huge stones, some at least thirteen paces long.

On one occasion Rab had allowed his courage to overcome his reason. By use of a well-tailored robe, "borrowed" from a local merchant, he had gotten into the Fortress through the less controlled southwestern entrance. He hoped to learn more about the area, thinking the information might someday be useful.

Rab had been duly impressed with the nearly smooth floor brought up to grade by thousands of huge white stones. In spite of his bravery he had known better than to venture near the soldier's barracks laid out in exact military fashion along the northern perimeter. And he stayed well clear of the huge guard towers on each corner. He had chosen instead to mingle with the merchants, lawyers, and the occasional priest in the central section. Rab had really concentrated in order to commit as much as possible of what he saw and felt to memory. But in spite of himself his mind kept admiring the beautiful buildings. He was tempted by his natural curiosity to venture inside the Roman temple, but even though he was not a religious Jew, he could not go that far.

Whether it is kosher to kill a Roman is a matter for discussion, Rab had thought, *but surely going into a pagan temple is not.*

Besides the military installations, Rab had wanted to see the judgment hall called the Praetorium. Over the years he had many of his friends taken up the hill to the Praetorium to stand trial. He had heard reports of their ascending the Rock where they would stand to answer the charges against them. The Rock was the literal pinnacle of Mt. Zion. The priests taught that the Rock was the actual place where Abraham had been commanded by God to offer his son, Isaac, as a sacrifice to prove his faith. Abraham had agreed and was about to slay his son when God produced a ram, caught in a bush. Supposedly, Isaac had come down from the Rock alive and God was given a new name, "Provider". But Rab could not recall a single one of his friends who had gone up to the Rock and come back down alive. None had ever been seen again.

Stories were rampant, but no one knew for sure. Undoubtedly, all had been scourged. In addition, a few had supposedly been sold as slaves to repay their debts to society. Others probably had been forced to become gladiators.

They are probably all dead by now, Rab cursed under his breath. *Evidently God chooses whom He will provide for.*

Rab thought of the various men he had known who had given their lives for the cause of freedom.

At least none have come down from the Rock just to be taken to a cross, Rab concluded. He glanced back at Jonah and then Isaac. *I wonder if we will be the first to enjoy that kind of Roman hospitality?*

A sudden shiver of fear coursed down his back along with the first drop of the perspiration that had suddenly begun to form on the back of his neck. Rab glanced up. The sun, still behind the Mount of Olives, was not hot enough to have brought it on.

To the rhythm of the chains on the stone street, Rab and his companions trudged forward. In an effort to push present and future reality from his mind, the thief retreated once more into his past. With a start of realization it occurred to Rab that he had actually never seen the Rock. His visit to the Fortress had been cut short. He had completed estimating the eastern and western walls to be approximately five hundred paces long, while the northern and southern walls of the rectangle were probably a little shorter. He had estimated there were barracks enough for five thousand Roman troops. He had seen the Roman Temple and had been deliberately moving toward the Praetorium.

Rab recalled, *Had I even flinched when those two young soldiers stopped me, I would have gotten a lot closer look at the Rock than I wanted.*

Rab almost laughed out loud as he remembered the two Romans. When they had asked his business he had simply smiled warmly and said he had come to bring a "gift" for a certain court magistrate but when he had arrived at the court, he had been told the judge was out of town. Thankfully, their suspicions had turned to larceny when he suggested that maybe the "gift" need not go to waste, whereupon he had produced from his nap sack a fairly expensive crock of wine.

Rab had seen enough, and so as the two soldiers walked away with their evening's libations, he had headed toward the nearest gate.

After all, he had joked with himself, *I can see the Praetorium with its famous Rock some other day.*

Rab was irritated by the increasing amount of sweat that was running down his spine.

Chapter Ten

Glancing sideways at the nearest soldier, Rab's heart sank. He realized that their approach to the Fortress, though a difficult climb, had only served to arouse the soldiers as well. His fears were confirmed as he looked from one to the other. Now instead of individuals taking a stroll, these men looked like a well trained unit on a mission, erect and alert.

"What a fool!" Rab scolded himself out loud. "What kind of threat am I?"

"I should have been looking for a way of escape instead of daydreaming," he said more to himself.

"What did you say?" Jonah's question caught the attention of the soldier nearest him.

"Shut up and keep moving," the soldier spit out, as he jabbed the end of his spear into Jonah's lower back. The youngest thief staggered and almost fell, but refused to respond verbally to the pain.

"Take it easy on the poor scum," the soldier on the other side of Jonah sneered as he grabbed Jonah's arm and jerked him back upright. The solder added, "You know this will probably be his last chance to enjoy such a nice morning walk."

Isaac, who had been knocked off both his pace and his prayers asked, "What's going on?"

"Just shut up and keep moving," the soldier nearest him growled.

Again the procession settled back into rhythmic routine. But in addition to the ring of the prisoner's chains keeping cadence with the soldiers' sandaled steps, the group now began to hear the noises of the awakening city. Soon the procession stopped in front of a large gate. It, like all on this western wall, was closed. There were two Temple soldiers guarding it, and they looked to Rab as if they had been up all night, but Rab knew they were coming to the end of only a three-hour watch. Though they were undoubtedly relieved to have something to do other than stand at attention, they acted somewhat put upon. One of the escort soldiers approached them, but their response was not what he had expected.

"I don't care who you are and what you're doing, I'm not going to open this gate until that sun is clearly above the Mount of Olives," the guard at the gate said, waving his spear toward the East. An argument ensued.

Pompous apes! Rab said to himself. He had observed these Temple soldiers and others like them for years. Though they were fellow Jews, they were little better than the Romans in their treatment of one another, much less the common man, but that did not explain the dispute. He then realized that they had been brought to a gate that was part of the colonnade between the Temple precinct and the Fortress. It was kind of a no-man's land which separated the Temple proper and courts to the south ruled by the Jews, from the Fort on the north ruled by the Romans. Even though Herod had built it, this middle section had seen more than its share of jurisdictional bickering. The fact that all of these soldiers were Jews working for the same system did not seem to matter.

As the discussion grew louder and more heated, Rab decided that if they ever were to escape, it had to be now. He noted that the two remaining guards had stepped forward to either observe or try to sway the argument. A quick look at Jonah revealed that he had been thinking the same thing as Rab. Even Isaac seemed alert, though fearful.

Rab quietly reached out with his left hand and took hold of the chain on his right wrist. He held it still as he signaled for his two friends to come closer. Keeping their eyes on the soldiers, Jonah and Isaac slid their feet closer to Rab, their chains barely making a sound on the stone street. When Rab figured they were close enough together to provide some slack in their chains, he motioned for them to kneel down.

Watching the soldiers and barely above a whisper Rab gave instructions, "Act tired. Stay close; back to back. Use the chains."

The thought of combat sent a wave of energy coursing through every part of Rab's body. From one to the other he looked his comrades in the eyes; his own burned with hatred for all in his life who had conspired to bring him to this place.

"If our blood has to flow today, then let it flow together with our enemies," Rab said through clenched teeth. Jonah's wild eyes and a toothy grin communicated his agreement. Isaac's eyes were almost as wide, and though his lips were moving rapidly, no sound was heard, at least by Rab.

The argument over jurisdiction had escalated until all but one of the soldiers was embroiled in it. That one glanced back at his prisoners. He was immediately aware that something was wrong. He could not be sure because the bound men were just outside the circle of light made by the torches mounted on the sides of the gate. Though the sky was beginning to lighten, the whole company was still in the western shadow of the massive stone wall. At best the prisoners were simply resting, but they had been alone long enough.

"Hey, what are you doing?" the soldier bellowed as he stepped back from the others and toward the three kneeling men. "Get up and spread out."

Isaac immediately started to stand, but one glance into his leader's eyes caused him to sink even lower. The other two acted as if they had either not heard the command or didn't care. They tried to portray that they were totally bored with the entire business. Out of the corner of his eye Rab observed the soldier moving toward him. Though his features were covered by his own shadow, Rab saw that as soldiers go, he was on the small size. Even his uniform was oversized and hung loosely on his body. Rab surmised that this man was not a soldier because he had earned the position. He certainly did not fit the physical profile. Rab hoped he didn't fair much better in the mental department. The thief had been around enough of these men to know that their jobs as personal guards of the High Priest were obtained purely through family, political or business connections. This guy was probably Caiaphas' second cousin or maybe a friend of a friend. Rab felt nothing but contempt for the fellow Jew. He was a weasel of a man. He was an enemy, and like the others, he was undoubtedly poorly trained.

It always amazed Rab how time seemed to slow down in moments like these. Every muscle and sinew in his body became tense with anticipation. His mind was fully alert. He knew the fire in his eyes was as concealed by the darkness as surely as the thoughts in his mind were concealed by another kind of darkness.

The soldier took two more steps toward the unmoving huddle, pointed the blunt end of his spear toward them in a motion designed to prod them to attention.

"It probably never occurred to you, my young soldier friend, that this is a good day to die."

The tenderness of the tone of voice was in such contrast to the content of the words that the soldier was momentarily confused. Unfortunately, he focused on the one speaking. Had he but glanced at the younger man, even the darkness would have not concealed the intent of his wicked grin.

"What did you say," the soldier asked, pressing the butt of his spear against the top back of Rab's left shoulder. The thief hunched forward as if to avoid the prod. The soldier responded by applying more pressure. The thief moved even lower but this time he reached up over his shoulder with his right hand, clasped the butt of the spear and jerked it forward with all his might. The startled soldier realized that his spear was slipping through his hands and immediately tried to tighten his grip. He found himself holding on to the spear's shaft with his arms fully extended. He barely had time to notice that the point of the spear was now aimed directly at his midsection.

Now with the shaft of the spear in both hands, Rab pulled downward with all the strength he could muster. His shoulders acted as a fulcrum. As he stood up, the soldier, still holding on to the business end of the spear, was lifted completely off the ground by the strength in his own arms. For a split second he hung there, like one hanging from a tree limb. Just as he let go, Rab thrust the spear directly backward. Its point made contact precisely below the soldier's chin. The man's windpipe was severed and he died in silence.

The soldier was still erect when another of the guards looked around. At first, though the scene did not look right, it did not look completely wrong either. Only when the younger of the prisoners stood upright, reached out and took the dead guard's sword did an alarm go off in the soldier's brain.

"They're trying to escape!" He shouted.

His companions immediately turned to see the three prisoners taking positions around the fallen soldier. One had his spear, the other his sword and the third, closed the ranks behind them. For moments it looked as if the soldiers were completely at a loss for what to do. Stirring themselves, the original guard detail, now only three strong, took up defensive positions beside each other. They were immediately joined on each side by the two gate guards, their territorial dispute quickly forgotten.

Rab observed that though the soldiers had a two-man advantage, they were not sure what to do. He suspected they did not want to end up like their buddy, whose now fallen body seemed to be their major focus. Rab punched Jonah in the side and in unison they stepped forward over the lifeless body of the guard and toward the soldiers. The soldiers instinctively stepped back toward the gate.

Rab was encouraged by their cowardice.

"If you boys don't want to end up like your pal, I suggest you drop your ..."

As he spoke he and Jonah took another step forward. Before Rab could finish his sentence an alarm went off in his mind. Something was wrong. He looked quickly at Jonah who also seemed distracted. A piercing wail echoed in their ears and without warning their arms were pulled down toward their waists as Isaac, who had been pulled along by his chains, tripped on the fallen soldier and fell between them. The two prisoners struggled now simply to maintain their balance, but without success. Jonah cursed as he fell directly on to Isaac. Isaac's initial scream was stopped as his breath was squeezed out of him by Jonah on the top and the dead guard below. But it did not take him long to regain his breath.

Rab, the strongest of the three, was able to thrust the end of the spear to the ground beside the pile of bodies and keep himself from falling headlong into the pile. He found himself on his knees with the spear directed somewhat in the direction of the soldiers. However, because of the chains he could no longer extend his arms.

The pitiful picture in front of the soldiers inspired new courage. They immediately rushed the prisoners. As one parried the spear with his own, another kicked the kneeling man full in the face. The third then pulled the spear from his hands. All five then encircled the three prisoners and began alternately kicking them and punching them with the blunt ends of their spears. Long after the three had slumped into submission, the soldiers' emotions drove them on.

"Stop!"

The sound caused the soldiers to hesitate.

"I order you to stop!"

The five crazed guards looked into the face of a Roman soldier. Again they hesitated.

"You idiots, what is going on here?

"Keep out of this. We have a score to settle with these scum. They killed one of my men."

"Do you not recognize who I am, soldier?" the Roman said, a wry smile creeping across his face as torchlight gave way to sunlight.

Holding the fallen prisoners beneath their feet, the soldiers looked up. The Centurion's armor was now easily observable and his authoritarian manner allowed the Temple soldiers to relax. When the Centurion gestured toward one of his men, the guards stepped completely away from the prisoners. By now all had been completely surrounded by Roman soldiers and one of them was holding up the standard of the Procurator, Pontius Pilate. Every Jew knew this emblem with its Roman eagle. It was considered a graven image by the teachers of the law and Pilate's insistence on using it made even the most irreverent of Jews despise him as much as he surely despised them. Seeing it now struck fear into the hearts of the young Judean soldiers.

"Who are these men?" the Centurion wanted to know.

"These three are prisoners sent over from his Excellency the High Priest, Joseph Caiaphas, Sir," the ranking guard managed to answer. "We were told to escort them to his Excellency, the Governor."

In response to a gesture by the Centurion, the Roman soldiers shoved the Temple guards aside and jerked the three prisoners up on their feet. In turn, two held up a prisoner while a third struck each one in the stomach several times. Soon all three were again lying in crumpled heap surrounded by soldiers. Meanwhile the Centurion had been inspecting the dead soldier's body.

"Killed with his own spear." It was more a statement of fact than a question, but the Centurion looked in the direction of the ranking soldier. He involuntarily shrugged his shoulders, hoping to feign indifference, but knew he was probably communicating negligence instead.

Ignoring this and looking over to the prisoners the officer asked, "Which one of these three parasites did this?"

The soldiers stepped aside to give their commander access to the three men who were just beginning to stir.

"Stand them up," the Centurion barked. "Okay, which one of you killed this man?"

The officer walked toward the three. Rab looked straight ahead. Jonah's eyes followed the Centurion while Isaac could only look at the ground. None spoke. The officer asked again, this time more quietly. Again, no response.

"No matter," he continued. "The way I see it, all three of you will die anyway."

Chapter Eleven

The sun had finally shown itself over the Mount of Olives. Even so, because of the scuffle, the gate to the colonnade had not been opened at the appointed time of sunrise. One of the Temple soldiers made some kind of signal to those inside the gate and soon the smaller door in the gate creaked back on its hinges. The Centurion ordered his men to take charge of the prisoners. They were once again lined up in single file and pushed toward the small door. Each man had to lower his head as he stepped over the threshold.

"We may never get out of this now. Especially if that idiot, Pilate, gets his hands on us," Jonah said as the door was closed and bolted behind them.

"Shut up, Jonah, as long as we have life we have a chance," Rab said trying to sound brave. "If those Romans had not shown up when they did, we would have gotten away."

For the sake of his men, Rab, tried to sound more confident than he was. He knew the odds of their survival were greatly diminishing with every step they took. They were marched another hundred paces or so and were stopped at a heavily guarded door. As soon as they were ushered through the door Rab recognized the area as the ground floor of the guard tower, the very same one he had come into from the street on his scouting excursion to the Fort. He quickly glanced to his left and noticed the door he had once used. Rab knew that just beyond it was the street and he recalled how sweet the air smelled and the warmth of the sun felt the day he had burst out through it after nearly being caught roaming around the Fortress above.

He then looked at the stone stairways encircling the stone walls. There were two, built on opposite sides of the tower. They climbed their way up to the plaza above and even beyond to the tower. For a moment it looked as if they were going to be taken up the stairs, but the Centurion barked some orders and they were herded toward another door across from the one they had entered.

More orders and it was opened. The three prisoners were led into a large chamber lit by torches. Rab tried to count the steps and note each turn. But after several descents down stairwells and ascents in others, he lost track. Rab had known that the pavement area of the Fortress above was huge. Now it was becoming painfully obvious that the underbelly held multiple layers of the same, but without the sunlight.

Finally they were stopped beside a gate made of iron bars illuminated by two torches and guarded by two soldiers. After a brief exchange, the soldiers opened the gate and shoved the three prisoners through a doorway and then shut the massive door. Rab, Jonah and Isaac found themselves inside a room that seemed to be four or five paces long and maybe three or four paces wide. It was dark but occasionally a reflection from the torches at the guard position outside would catch a smooth enough section of the worn white stone walls to give them a brief look at their surroundings. The men still were chained together, and at first, they roamed around the room examining the walls with their free hands. Their movement resembled some strange dance. Each in turn discovered the iron loops built into the walls and each was thankful they had not been shackled to them, at least not yet. Isaac was the first to sit down on a pile of dirty straw someone had kicked against the wall. The others soon followed his lead. What choice did they have?

Rab finally spoke, "Well here we are, in the Fortress of Antonia. You've heard about it all your professional lives, now what do you think?"

His attempt to break the tension was ignored as was his question. Isaac was too tired and frightened to think, much less speak. He just sat still, his face buried in his hands. In contrast to Isaac's resignation, Jonah was seething with anger. He was like a volcano about to explode but for once in his life he chose to hold it in. Especially since the one he was angry toward was sitting, shackled next to him. Jonah believed that if Isaac had not fallen down, they would have won their freedom. He also knew they were either going to spend the rest of their lives in this room, or one like it, or they were going to die ... all because of Isaac. He had never wanted to kill anyone so much in all his blood stained life. But he also knew that either the Romans would take care of that for him or there would be plenty of time for him to do it. He just concentrated on controlling his breathing.

Rab had no idea how long they would be in this place. He tried to think back over the accounts he had heard of his friends who had been captured by the Romans. Had they been allowed visitors who had told of an initial holding area where they were kept before facing trial? He thought so and, of course, he knew the Romans prided themselves in their system of laws.

Surely, we will receive a fair trial, He reflected. *At least I will get to see, even stand on, the Rock where Father Abraham stood.*

He started to share his thoughts with Jonah and Isaac, but stopped short when he had to admit that neither of the suggestions gave him much comfort.

Then, for the first time he noticed he had been rubbing his hands. It was as if he had been trying to remove something from them. Again, he rubbed them, first one and then the other. But what was on them? In the near darkness, the substance caked on Rab's hands appeared dark, darker than his own skin. Whatever it was, it was vaguely familiar. Just then someone passed through a distant doorway creating a slight breeze which fanned the torchlight just enough for it to reflect into his cell. There! He could see it now. It was dark and brown, and despite his best efforts, it still covered most of both his hands. Another flicker and Rab knew. It wasn't brown at all, but dark red.

Blood ... blood on my hands, he thought. *That's not so unusual, I have had much blood on my hands. So what!* Just then a new thought screamed for recognition. *Jewish blood,* he winced, *I have Jewish blood on my hands!*

Suddenly, sitting on the cold stone floor, despite being shackled by iron chains to the only friends he had in world, Jesus Bar-Abbas felt totally alone.

A deep heaviness settled over him heavier than any blanket he had known. Just when he thought he could endure the darkness of his own soul no longer, something wrenched inside of him. It was as if he had been thrown from a ship into the midst of a stormy sea, his whole being was flooded with wave after wave of dark, suffocating emotion. A lifetime of feelings of rejection, fear, hatred and evil found him in that dark room. Harsh words spoken in anger, faces gnarled in hatred, the last gasps of young soldiers far away from home, bitter thoughts of missed opportunities, evil choices made and deeds even more evil done all pressed themselves upon his mind and heart. As hard as he tried to will the images and feelings to go away, they would not. It was out of sheer physical exhaustion that Rab finally found relief through sleep, but not entirely. Even his dreams were haunted.

Chapter Twelve

"Hey, Rab! Rab! Wake up!" It was Jonah.

"Come on, man, you're scaring us half to death," Jonah was nearly shouting as he shoved his leader once more in the shoulder. "You've got to stop ranting about blood on your hands. If anybody hears that kind of talk we're all as good as crucified."

Rab jerked to an upright position and though he recognized Jonah's voice, for an instant he was not sure of anything else, where he was or what time it was. Years of the practice of just staying alive kept him from asking. Instead he waited for his mind to clear and his senses to return.

"You woke me up with all that ..." Jonah began again. "Hey, that hurts!"

Rab had located Jonah's chain and had given it a sharp jerk, pulling the smaller man so close he could smell, if not feel, Jonah's breath.

"You don't know hurt yet," Rab scowled in the young thief's direction, jerking the chain once more.

But this time the chain did not move, but was jerked back. Rab immediately realized that Jonah was not giving in as usual. The muscles in Rab's body instantly tightened. His powerful hands closed on the chain stopping its movement. As his body came to life, so did his brain. His senses searched the darkness for clues about his comrade and potential opponent. But everything was quiet.

He is holding his breath so as not to give away his position, Rab smiled to himself. In a way that he could not understand because he had never had a son of his own, the fact that Jonah had learned his lessons well awakened a bit of consolation, even pride in Rab.

After what seemed a long time, but was only a few seconds, Rab felt the tension on the chain relax. When he heard it land on the floor, he too relaxed his grip, but he himself remained alert. Finally Jonah spoke.

"I'm sorry, Rab. I didn't mean to make you mad, but I was afraid your hollering was going to bring one of those guards in here. That's all."

The words were right, but Jonah couldn't hide his anger – or was it fear?

"Don't worry about the guards," Rab tried to sound confident, but he was still shaken by his poor performance. "We can handle those guys."

"I'm glad you think so, but I've got to tell you this place gives me the creeps," Jonah replied, beginning to calm down. "I thought the High Priest's cellar was bad, but, man ..." His voice trailed off into the darkness, then after an extended pause he added, "they can kill you in here, right?"

"Yeah, but like I told that stupid soldier, 'This is a good day to die,'" Rab answered with intended conviction.

"That sounded good out there, but it sounds crazy in here." Jonah suddenly released his emotion, "I don't want to die in here and I don't want to die today." After a short pause he added, "I ain't ready to die, not here, not now, not me!"

Isaac, who had been quiet through all of this suddenly began to pray, "O God, have mercy on our souls. We are sinners, O God; we don't deserve Your mercy but we need it. Have mercy on us, O God."

"You better pray for mercy, you old fool," Jonah smirked. "If the Romans don't kill you, I'll do it myself. It's your fault we're in here in the first place."

At that, Isaac shuffled around toward the wall and lowered his voice. Though he continued to pray, his prayers could no longer be understood.

Rab was surprised at his own reaction to this. He was actually sorry that he could no longer understand Isaac's prayers. He had never had much use for God, but for some reason, Isaac's prayers had resonated with feelings and longings deep within him.

"O God, have mercy on me a sinner," Rab said in a whisper that he could not even hear with his own ears. He dare not let Jonah hear, but inwardly he hoped it was loud enough for God to hear.

Chapter Thirteen

"Wake up! Get up! Hurry up, let's go," the soldier commanded as he pushed and prodded Rab into first a sitting position and then to his feet.

"Use that spear on him if he moves," the soldier said as he bent down to release Rab from the chains on his feet. "Secure those other two and let's get going; we can't keep the Governor waiting," the lead soldier barked orders as he placed a new set of iron shackles on Rab's feet and then attached them with a chain to those still on his wrists.

After the cold darkness of the cell, even the warm light from the torches forced Rab to squint his eyes as he stumbled through the door into the stone hallway. He was disoriented, and for a while wondered what time it was, or for that matter, what day it was. But then a more bizarre question began to form.

Governor! Did that soldier say, 'Governor'?

As he was shoved toward the first set of stairs Rab tried to push the thought out of his mind so he could again concentrate on counting the ascending steps. A perpetual sense of hope of living another day required him to at least consider that he might need to find his way back down to where his friends were being held. But his mind would not let go of the comment about the Governor any more than his legs would let go of the sharp needle pricks that came from lack of circulation. Try as he might, Rab could not make his mind work much better than his body. He finally gave up trying to figure it out, just as he gave up counting the steps. With each set of stone stairs brought more illumination and the next hallway. Finally he was thrust through the doorway leading up and onto the pavement of the Fortress of Antonia. The sunlight was blinding, but the air was warm and sweet with the fragrance of life floating up from the olive groves across the Kidron valley.

It is a good day, Rab thought, b*ut not to die*, he concluded as a cloud of gloom as dark as the dungeon he had just left descended upon him.

Rab hardly noticed the pain as the soldiers prodded him along. Instead, he began to notice those who were stopping their activities to watch as he was pushed and pulled through the crowded market area. As his eyes adjusted he found himself looking at those he passed, even as they were looking at him. He had seen all this before, but it was as if he were seeing it for the very first time. Maybe it was an experience that all condemned, or soon to be condemned men had, but Rab actually looked at the faces and then into the eyes of each person he encountered.

He briefly wondered about each one: *Who are you? Where are you from? Why are you in this place? What are you trying to do here? Does anyone love you or care whether you live or die? Or are you, like me, just trying to survive?*

Another wave of dark emotion settled over Rab as he realized that so much of his life had been wasted on issues and activities that now at this moment seemed so pointless. Even the few friendships he had formed over the years had been for his own convenience or to accomplish some less than honorable exercise. People had been objects to be used.

"God, forgive me ... I am a sinner," Rab heard himself say.

The soldiers heard him too. "Not likely any god is going to hear you today. Don't you know its feast day and they are all busy. Anyway, surely even the Jewish gods don't have time for the likes of you. You had just better hope the Roman gods don't get a hold of you," the soldier laughed in derision as he jerked the prisoner to a halt.

Rab glanced quickly at the sun and determined from its position just sneaking over the Mount of Olives that it must still be early in the first watch of the day, maybe seven o'clock. Despite himself, Rab winced as the skin on his arm was pinched as the soldiers pushed him forward once more. Rab now realized the trappings and ornamentation of his Jewish kinsmen had given way to that of the legions of Rome. He was stopped once more as the soldier in charge of his detachment sharply saluted a superior. The officer turned immediately and spoke to an even higher ranking officer. Rab had never seen so many Roman officers in one place in all his life, one of whom he noted was the Centurion who had stopped their escape. Before the familiar feelings of rage could surface, his attention was diverted beyond the cadre of soldiers to a solitary individual standing on the porch of one of the buildings.

Rab had never actually seen Pontius Pilate before and so he was not completely certain that the man he now saw was in fact the Governor. But the soldier had said the Governor wanted to see him. Maybe it was true. At any rate, the mere idea of a man with his own background, not to mention his reputation, being brought before the Roman Governor struck dread into Rab's already plagued heart. Time seemed to be rushing by. Rab looked once more at the sun, but it seemed to have not moved.

Suddenly Rab, who had sent numerous men into eternity now knew that he himself was facing his eternity. He, who had with merciless cruelty acted as both judge and executioner to many, now was convinced that apart from a miracle of the God he barely believed in, he would soon face that same God as his Judge. All of the noble reasons he had given himself and others over the years for his many crimes now seemed absolutely ridiculous, even in his own mind.

Even so, because of his training, Rab managed to maintain his outward composure, but on the inside it was all he could do to keep from becoming sick. More out of rote than thought, like a cornered animal he again began a desperate search of the area to find a weakness in his enemy, a way of escape. Within the next few moments he concluded he would find neither, not with so many Roman soldiers present. But in those same moments he made another discovery.

Chapter Fourteen

Rab looked once more at Pontius Pilate who was acting anything but the way the thief imagined a governor should. He was gesturing wildly as he paced back and forth on what may have been the front porch of his house, or was it the Praetorium? Rab looked to see whom he was addressing. Even from his poor vantage point behind what looked like a whole company of Roman soldiers, the ceremonial robes of the Jewish Court were easily recognizable. They were the most ornamental in the nation. There always seemed to be some effort on their part, especially at festival time, to see who could come up with the most elaborate dress. Even now Rab held them all in contempt. Then for the second time he saw the High Priest. Now he knew his fate was sealed. The High Priest had promised to turn him over to Pilate.

Rab looked back at the Governor just as Pilate looked toward Rab and gestured. The Centurion barked an order and soldiers in front parted as others on each side pressed the thief into motion. Rab suddenly felt the strength leave his knees. He tried to walk, but his feet felt as if they were mired in clay. He was disgusted with his own weakness. Another order from the Centurion and two additional soldiers stepped up and together the four dragged Rab forward. Instead of moving him directly toward the Governor, they jerked Rab to his left. As he staggered forward, the last rank of what must have been Pilate's personal guard stepped aside leaving the way open for him to see his destination: the Pavement Stone. He was going to the Rock. In spite of himself, Rab was grateful to have a couple of Roman soldiers holding on to each of his arms. He tried to use the arising self-condemnation to motivate himself to face this moment with some measure of dignity, if not courage. He decided to focus on the Rock, but as he approached the first step, the soldiers suddenly stopped him and turned him around to face the priests.

Rab was surprised to see how many priests were

present. It looked like the entire Sanhedrin. Beyond them was an even larger crowd of Jewish citizens. He recognized many of the men as shop owners and temple traders, relatives and cronies of the priests. Rab's thoughts began to whirl as he realized these were the very same group of hustlers he had tried unsuccessfully to buy his way into.

What are these men doing here? What could motivate them to leave their shops during one of the most lucrative times in the year?" he puzzled. *Have they come here to testify against me?* The very thought both angered and nauseated him.

When the priests and the crowd behind them noticed Rab's arrival they lifted up a shout. It was so loud that Rab could not tell the purpose of it. Some actually looked glad to see him, like he was a long lost friend, but others showed real hostility.

Before the thief could make any sense of it, the soldiers once again tightened their grips on his arms. They turned him to the right and pushed him onto the steps leading up to the Rock.

The judgment has come, thought Rab, hardly noticing the soldiers' rough prodding as he struggled up the steps.

But before he reached the top, the crowd once more began to shout. This time their discordant screams coalesced into a single cry which swelled to a chant.

"Crucify him! Crucify him! Crucify him!" they shouted in chorus as if rehearsed and orchestrated.

Rab could feel hatred wash over him like a dry wind off the Dead Sea in the heat of summer. It all but took his breath. As his energy drained, the hypocrisy of it all was not lost. He knew these men to be thieves, conspirators and undoubtedly, even murders. Was he paying for their guilt?

He dared to take his eyes off the steps long enough to glare at the angry crowd. To his complete astonishment they were not even looking at him nor were their angry gestures being made in his direction. They were not even looking at

Pilate. Their focus was on something or someone else. What or whoever was the focus of their wrath must have been directly on the other side of the Rock.

The soldiers gave the thief one final push. Just as Rab stepped onto the top step, he spotted the man standing on the pavement just below the other side of the Stone.

Rab was more startled than he was surprised to see Jesus, the other Jesus from Pilate's prison. Then Rab remembered, the high priest had said he would see them both brought before Pilate.

Something had changed about Jesus and at first, Rab could not determine just what it was. Then he realized, instead of the blood soaked garment Jesus had been wearing in the prison, he was now clothed in a very ornamental robe.

That's no cheap robe, the thief observed in spite of his situation. *What is he doing wearing that?*

Then on closer examination Rab noticed that what he had thought was decoration on the shoulders of the kingly purple robe was in fact dried blood. For the first time he looked at Jesus' face. Rab had thought the claim-to-be Messiah's face had been badly beaten before, but he now saw that the swelling was even worse, and so was the bleeding. And what was that on his head? It looked like a wreath of some kind, but it was larger than a traditional victory crown and it wasn't green, but dark brown, and jagged.

It's a crown ... made out of thorns, Rab realized, *and that's the cause of the bleeding; someone has placed that on his head and pushed it down, or beaten it down, into his scalp.*

Then Rab realized that the whole costume had been designed to mock Jesus and his claim to be the Son of God, the King of a New Kingdom.

Obviously, no king with any true authority would allow these Jewish phonies or these Roman infidels to treat him with such disrespect and cruelty. Immediately the feelings of hatred that had begun to focus in the prison once again exploded into Rab's mind.

"Well, it looks like someone has taken your claim to be a king seriously," Rab almost spat the words at Jesus as the soldiers pushed the two prisoners toward one another.

At first there was no indication to Rab that Jesus had even heard his words, much less that they wounded him as he had intended. But just as both the prisoners were being turned by the soldiers to face the crowd, Jesus looked directly into Rab's eyes, and to Rab's amazement, instead of anger or hatred or even pain, Rab saw once more a depth of compassion that, if anything, was now even greater than it had been in Caiaphas' prison. The look of love confused Rab and the thief hated Jesus even more for it.

"Don't look at me like that," Rab said as he turned his gaze toward the crowd. "If it hadn't been for you, I would not be standing here today. You ruined my life. It's your fault my parents were killed. As far as I'm concerned they can hang you on the nearest cross, and if they would take these shackles off, I would drive the nails myself."

Before there was any reply from Jesus, the crowd which had divided itself into various groups, most of which were embroiled in angry discussions, suddenly came to order and to a man, focused their attention toward the two prisoners standing on either side of the Rock. A whirl of emotion embroiled Rab, and it took all his strength to maintain any sense of composure. Rab was relieved when Pontius Pilate began to wave his arms to quiet the crowd.

"Behold the Man!"

A roar went up from the crowd. Again Pilate waved his arms for quiet.

"You brought this man to me as one who incites the people to rebellion," Pilate began.

A feeling of weakness once again swept through Rab's knees.

"And behold, having examined Him before you," Pilate continued, "I have found no guilt in this man regarding the charges which you make against him."

Instantly a collective groan of protest swept through the crowd. Rab was even more confused. Pilate raised his voice just slightly and continued to speak.

"In addition, I sent Him to be examined by King Herod. King Herod questioned Him, found no fault with Him, and sent Him back to me."

At this several in the crowd began to hiss, but Pilate continued. "And nothing deserving death has been done by Him."

Now the murmurs began to increase and some in the crowd began shouting, "No! No! No!"

The rest of the crowd picked up the words and they soon became a chant, "No! No! No!"

Rab was totally confused now. On one hand he knew he had not been sent to Herod, at least not yet, but on the other hand the Governor was declaring him innocent. In addition, he could not understand the crowd's hostility. Sure he had stolen a few coins over the years, but ...?

Pilate allowed the crowd to continue for some time. When the crowd noise finally began to subside a little, Pilate concluded, "Therefore I will punish him and release him."

The crowd exploded in fury.

Rab watched as suddenly, the Roman soldiers who had been placed mainly to the sides now moved into a defensive position between Jesus and himself and the crowd. Once in place, they brought their spears forward to the ready. This time Rab noticed that it was the Centurion who had signaled them.

Rab could barely hear himself think.

What is going on here? he wondered, his mind racing.

Someone in the crowd hollered out, "Kill Him and release Bar-Abbas to us!" Instantly the whole crowd picked up the chant, "Kill Him and release Bar-Abbas to us! Kill Him and release Bar-Abbas to us! Kill Him and release Bar-Abbas to us," they thundered.

The soldiers were becoming obviously nervous as the crowd, in their agitation, moved forward toward the Stone with its two prisoners. Another signal from the Centurion and the soldiers protecting them drew in closer.

All the while the Governor tried to reason with the crowd. He was now shouting, "I find no fault in Him!"

It finally dawned on Rab that Pilate wanted to release Jesus, but the crowd, quickly becoming a mob, shouted back, "Crucify Him! Crucify Him!"

The situation began to crystallize in Rab's mind. He had all but forgotten that the Romans liked to believe they were tolerant and merciful rulers. To prove it, each year at festival time, the Governor would release a prisoner. Although Rab had always seen this as hypocritical, it had proven to be a valuable political tool. Plus he had been pleased that some of his fellow 'freedom fighters' had regained their own freedom which meant they could fight another day.

Now Rab realized that Pilate wanted to release Jesus but the crowd wanted the Governor to release him. He suddenly felt a surge of energy rise up from deep within himself. "Crucify Him! Crucify Him!" Rab joined in, turning to glare at Jesus.

Again Pilate tried to quiet the crowd. "Why? What crime has He committed? I have no reason to put Him to death. I will have Him flogged and then release Him."

"No!" Rab instantly shouted.

And just as quickly the crowd joined in. "No! No! Crucify Him! Crucify Him!"

Rab turned toward Pilate in time to see him shrug his shoulders and turn and give orders to one of his attendants who immediately stepped away. The attendant returned shortly with a basin and towel. Rab watched as Pilate turned to the crowd and began washing his hands.

"I am innocent of this man's blood. The responsibility is yours!"

The High Priest shouted, "His blood be on our heads and on our children's!"

The crowd immediately picked up the chant, "His blood be on our heads and on our children's!"

Waving the attendant aside, Pilate looked one more time at the crowd, shrugged his shoulders, and then turned and gave orders to the Centurion, loud enough for everyone to hear, "Release Jesus Bar-Abbas! Have Jesus the Nazarene flogged and then ... crucify Him!"

Chapter Fifteen

The possibility of his own death was a constant in Rab's line of work, but one that he usually managed to keep out of his consciousness. This morning Rab had not only faced it, but it had nearly brought him to his knees in fear. Now, that fear was slowly draining out of him. He was numb - stunned. For a brief moment Rab wondered if all this had been a nightmare from which he was waking. He had certainly had many of those in which he descended into deep darkness with seemingly no way out, only to awaken as the first rays of a new day broke into his consciousness.

He slowly became aware that a man was standing in front of him. The glare in the eyes of the Roman Centurion could have melted steel, and so Rab merely feigned indifference. He also tried to ignore the shoving he was receiving from the three soldiers who were taking off his shackles. Rab was not comfortable being so close to such a high ranking officer, especially the officer in charge of the Governor's personal body guard. He had stared down some of the most malevolent criminal types in Jerusalem, but this man's contempt was obvious and Rab made a mental note to remember his face in case some future opportunity for justice presented itself. Through it all, the thief's mind, as well as his gaze was beginning to make some sense out of the change in his legal status.

He reacted little to the rougher than necessary prods as the Romans pushed him, first down and then away from the Rock. He stumbled as they gave him one final shove, but their warnings to leave the area did not strike home. Rubbing his wrists, he had taken only a step or two away when the Governor's words echoed back into his consciousness. "Release Jesus Bar-Abbas ..." He had just received a pardon from Pilate.

That's the same as a pardon from Caesar himself, Rab rehearsed until it became a reality for him.

"I'm free! No one can touch me" he said aloud. He was walking back the way he had come, along the line of Roman soldiers still forming a barrier between the crowd and the Governor. None of them seemed to embrace his joy.

"You better watch yourself," one of the soldiers hissed through clenched teeth.

The next one added, "That pardon is only good for past crimes. You'll be back."

Rab knew the soldiers were fighting their inner desire to dispense Roman justice to him on the spot. And at this moment as much as he hated the Romans he did appreciate their military discipline. Still he did not let his guard down as he made his way from the Praetorium. He was nearing the end of the line of soldiers when he heard the crowd behind him raise up a loud shout, "One!"

Then a moment later, "Two!"

Rab looked back.

"Three!" "Four!"

In his haste to get away from the Praetorium he had completely forgotten about the religious leaders and the mob of citizens that surrounded them.

"Jesus," whispered Rab. He had also forgotten about Jesus. "They're flogging Jesus."

Despite his desire to get to a safer place, he could not. His reawakened courage was bolstered by the hatred he had for Jesus. The thought of that false messiah being flogged brought a smile to Rab's face. He turned around and started back toward the crowd and their focus just beyond the Rock.

The mob-like crowd was now cheering every stroke of the lictor's swing of the flagellum.

"Eleven!" "Twelve!" "Thirteen!"

Rab had seen a few public scourges, but never up close. He had seen the gruesome results up close. A number of his colleagues had endured that particular punishment, perfected by the Romans and used on the vilest offenders, and usually on those to be crucified: women, senators and soldiers, except deserters, were exempt.

"Sixteen!" "Seventeen!" "Eighteen!" "Nineteen!"

Rab was now close enough to hear the cracks of the whip and the slaps and thuds of the cords hitting flesh. He could also hear the muffled cries of Jesus following every swing of the flagellum.

Rab and his friends had often discussed the Roman flagellum, or whip. It was a devilish creation. It was made of nine strands of leather attached to a wooden handle. The nine cords gave it is common name: cat o' nine tails. Being whipped by the rawhide ropes would have been painful enough, but the real damage was done by what was attached to them. Sharp pieces of sheep bone were sewn into each strand and heavy iron balls were tied to the ends. With each lash, a skilled lictor would bruise the deep muscles of the back with the iron balls and rip the surface muscles with the leather and bone fragments. Scourges were limited to thirty-nine lashes because it was believed that forty lashes meant certain death.

"Twenty-two!" "Twenty-three!" "Twenty-four!"

Rab knew the goal was to weaken the criminal so that if he survived he would never be a threat again and if he was to be crucified, he would die a horrible death, but in a reasonable time. The lictors, were chosen for their strength and their ability to learn to weld the whip with precision and restraint. One misplaced lash could penetrate the shredded muscle, rip into the abdominal cavity, rip out a kidney, lung or other vital organ and cause instant death. That would eliminate the crucifixion and rob the crowd of their sadistic entertainment and the Romans of the example they made to would be offenders of Roman law. Even so, the most skilled practitioner knew that half of all he flogged would die within a week or two from breathing problems. Those who did live through the beating, and not scheduled for crucifixion, would be crippled for life.

None of my friends have ever walked upright again,

Rab thought as he brashly forced his way to the front of the crowd. Besides their natural reflexes to being brushed past, no one even gave him so much as a glance. Their focus was entirely on the scene before them.

"Twenty-eight!" "Twenty-nine!" The crowd continued to count.

Despite Rab's knowledge of scourging, he was not prepared for what he was now able to see. Before him was a totally naked man with his hands stretched upward and tied by ropes so that he embraced a tall, large pole. Rab could not see Jesus' face because his head sagged against the pole. His feet were barely touching the ground and his back was fully exposed, to the crowd and to the soldier who was now moving around to the prisoner's other side.

The soldier, probably another Centurion Rab supposed, was sprinkled from head to toe with blood. Jesus' back looked to Rab as if it had been shredded with a hundred knife strokes. Several segments of white ribs were showing, their gray sheathing ripped away. His blood, running down and dripping from both legs, was darkening as it filled the cracks and pooled on the dusty stone pavement.

"Thirty-two!" "Thirty-three!" "Thirty-four!"

Rab had joined in the counting, and like others now was doing so less enthusiastically with each swing of the whip. The sight was almost sickening, even to a hardened heart such as his. In order to steel himself, Rab recalled his promise to Jesus that if given the chance he would drive the crucifixion nails himself. Now his hatred was faltering with each rip of flesh and cry of anguish. He had to compose himself.

That's right, he realized. *That could have been me. And it's his fault!*

"Don't stop, you Roman! Do your job! Swing that cat! He has it coming!" Rab screamed above the crowd. "He's getting what he deserves"

"Thirty-seven!" "Thirty-eight!"

The lictor stopped to catch his breath and possibly to admire his handiwork or maybe determine whether or not to continue or if so which side of the once strong man before him could endure one more swing of the nine-tailed whip.

"Don't stop! You're not finished, you weakling!"

The Centurion paused. He looked at Bar-Abbas, the muscles in his face tensing as he recognized the recently pardoned murderer. Wiping blood from his eyes with the back of his leathered wrist, he took a step toward Bar-Abbas and said, "This should be you, you ungrateful piece of dung!"

Rab only wagged his head as the soldier turned back and with one final swing finished his gruesome task.

"Aaahhhh!" Jesus winced.

"Thirty-nine!" the crowd bellowed.

Chapter Sixteen

The show was over, at least for most of the crowd. They began to file away. Shop owners back to the shops, accountants and lawyers back to their offices, but the priests stayed and so did Bar-Abbas. He knew that the flogging was only the beginning of the death of Jesus who called Himself the Messiah. He also knew the Roman soldiers, being far away from home on a tour of duty they despised, would pour out the full fury of their inner pain on their hapless prisoner.

Sure enough, Rab watched as they cut the ropes attached to his wrists. Jesus fell into a mass of bleeding skin and shredded muscles. One of the soldiers took a crock of water and threw it on Him. Without a hint of human compassion, two other soldiers lifted Him to His feet and held Him while a couple of others once again placed the kingly robe on Him and then, a bit more carefully, the crown of thorns on His head. They handed Jesus a spear with the head broken off.

Probably to represent a scepter, thought Rab.

As Jesus steadied Himself with the spear, all of the soldiers now joined in as they marched around Him shouting praises, "Hail to the King!" "Long live the new King!"

Several of those still watching, joined the mockery. Rab was about to join the raucous chorus when the officer in charge, the Centurion, stepped between him and the spectacle.

Looking directly into Rab's eyes, the officer smiled and said just loud enough for Rab to hear, "You do realize how fortunate you are? The fates have smiled on you today. You ought to go over to that man and fall down and kiss His feet. He is taking your place! If He had not been here, that would be you."

Rab heard what the officer said, but could not determine why he had said it, not that he cared. The thief was glad he had been spared this horrible treatment and the crucifixion to follow, but in his mind the phony Messiah had it coming, if for no other reason than for how He had messed up his life. *No telling how many others He has harmed.*

The Centurion glanced up at the sun as a reminder that time was passing. He then gave the order to prepare Jesus for crucifixion. The soldiers shrugged, steadied Jesus, took off the crown of thorns and then ripped the now blood-soaked robe from His back. Even the jaded crowd winced as the clotting mass of blood on Jesus' back tore loose and once more began to bleed freely.

After placing Jesus' own robe, now brown with dried blood, back on Him, two soldiers held Him up while two others brought a beam of wood and laid it on His shoulders. They raised His arms and tied His wrists to the heavy timber.

With a wicked grin one soldier said, "I hear you are a carpenter's son. You should be able to carry a small piece of wood like this."

The instant they stopped holding up the beam, Jesus took a few small steps to balance Himself under the heavy load. Realizing He could not manage, He stumbled over to the flogging pole and leaned against it.

"Amazing," said the soldier. "You're the first one on my duty that has not fallen. Maybe you were a carpenter. But you sure don't look like a king," he laughed in derision.

The Centurion barked orders to his squad, "Bring the other two thieves and let's get this operation moving."

One of the soldiers ran toward the barracks and repeated the commander's orders.

In a moment another soldier came out of the building, turned and waited. Rab watched as another man tried to make his way through the door. The soldier went back, turned the man sideways and pulled on one of His arms. The problem soon became obvious.

"That man is also carrying a crossbeam," observed Rab to no one in particular. "He must be one of the other men to be crucified today."

Suddenly the blood drained from his face and his legs went limp.

"Jonah, Jonah is that you? Oh no. Is that you?" Rab shouted and started to run toward his young friend. Three soldiers immediately caught and threw him face down on the ground. It took several seconds for him to realize that the soldiers were not going to let him up until he stopped struggling. Finally he allowed his muscles to go limp, and he just lay there trying his best to see what had happened to his young Jonah.

When the soldiers realized he had stopped resisting them, they turned him over, gave him a strict warning to get back. When they saw he was compliant, they picked him up and pushed him back toward the crowd.

Rab quickly turned back around in time to see Isaac being helped through the doorway out into the morning sun. His foot slipped and under the weight of the heavy crosspiece he would have fallen if he hadn't been caught by the soldiers.

"Oh no! Not Isaac too! Oh!"

Turning in the direction of the Centurion Rab shouted, "Please, please, not Isaac. He is a simple old man who means no harm to anyone. He doesn't deserve to die."

The Centurion spun around to Rab with a look that could have killed. He started to speak, then paused a moment.

"Well, really? I suppose you want to volunteer to take his place?" the officer asked with a wicked smile. "I mean what are friends for?"

The words sank deep as Rab turned to watch the soldiers herd the stumbling Jonah and Isaac toward the flogging post. First the soldiers flogged Jonah, then Isaac. Rab could barely watch. His only solace was that they had spent most of their energy on Jesus and so Jonah's beating was less severe. By the time they got to Isaac, they had lost their stomach for it and the officer allowed them to cut the savage beating short. When they were finished, the soldiers guarding Jesus pulled Him upright, turned Him toward the crowd and gave Him a shove.

The Centurion made sure his small entourage was in order: three soldiers up front, one carrying the execution orders and two with spears. Next came the three criminals, Jesus first, then Isaac followed by Jonah, accompanied by two soldiers each. Two more soldiers served as a rear guard walked right in front of the officer.

"Let's go!" he ordered. "It's a good day to die."

Chapter Seventeen

Golgotha, Hebrew for Place of the Skull, was the destination. Bar-Abbas knew it well. Everyone did. It was a rocky hill just across the main road near the Benjamin Gate on the north wall of Jerusalem. Most believed its name came from the fact that its sheer rock wall contained several small caves, which when viewed from a short distance gave the hill the appearance of a skull. Bar-Abbas thought it was named that because of all the skulls, and other human bones, lying around from unclaimed, crucified criminals. The Romans always crucified criminals in public places where many people would be forced to see them. The top of Golgotha, or Calvaria, as the Romans called it, was ideal.

Bar-Abbas watched as the soldiers opened the large gates in the western wall protecting the Fortress and the small group moved out, those to be crucified straining under the weight of their crossbeams, with the soldiers prodding them along. Most of the crowd had filtered away but a few of the priests were following along. Rab was not sure what to do - follow the procession or go find someone to help. It had occurred to him that he might be able to ambush and overpower the squad of soldiers and break Isaac and Jonah free. He would leave Jesus, of course, to His just outcome. While trying to think of a better plan, Rab followed a few steps behind.

Compared to the bright sunlight of the Fortress, the small street outside the western wall of the Fortress was still in the shade. The cool air was a welcome relief to Rab and he hoped it was to Isaac and Jonah as well. As he glanced at Jesus he saw a different picture. Jesus was now shivering violently.

"Evidently," Rab observed, "His sweat, along with the massive loss of blood from His gaping wounds, has super cooled His body." He could not help but admire the man's strength.

He is bearing up under the weight of that crossbeam as well as Jonah, better than Isaac. I wonder how much longer He will be able to go on?

For a moment he thought about starting a wager on which of the three would collapse under the pressure first and considered whether he could capitalize on this bizarre situation.

"You idiot!" he scolded himself aloud. He suddenly realized he had attracted the attention of the soldiers. He looked away and finished his tirade silently. *What kind of man thinks about making money at the expense - expense nothing, the suffering and death of his only friends?*

Again he looked at Jesus. *It's your fault I am such a vile person. You made me this way. At least you are getting what you deserve.*

The relatively small number of people on the street right outside the wall had obviously not heard that a crucifixion was taking place. Most were women who lived nearby. Rab could see the shock on their faces as the group approached. The men in the city were already or would soon be busy preparing the lambs for the Passover sacrifices and family meals that would happen all over the city later in the day. Rab could not help but notice that the few men who were present had smiles on their faces. Some poked and jabbed elbows at each other.

No doubt these are the remainder of the group hired by the priests to persuade Pilate to choose Jesus over me to be crucified, Rab decided with a mixture of relief, admiration and contempt. *Quite a day for them*, he concluded. *They get rid of a couple of bothersome thieves and a troublesome preacher, and get paid for their troubles as well.*

Young boys now began to run ahead with the news of the crucifixion and soon, Rab knew, a crowd would be gathering. The small street they were now on, El Wad, took them northwestward toward the Benjamin Gate. As the procession made its way, more and more onlookers gathered in front of the stores on both sides of the street. Rab half expected the gawkers to treat this somewhat like a parade, given the fact that this was the middle of the Feast of Passover and many Jews were in town from all over the world, enjoying the festivities and seeing the sights. No doubt many had heard of Roman crucifixions and wondered what one would be like. But if the onlookers were tempted to take the event lightly, one look at Jesus and the struggling thieves sobered them quickly. Rab noticed most of their attention seemed to be focused on Jesus. His blood-soaked robe and crown of thorns evoked expressions of compassion for many, anger from some and confusion from most.

"What an irony!" Rab thought. "Here we are in the middle of a celebration of freedom from slavery from the Egyptians and we have to endure the indignity of slavery to the Romans. When will we ever be free? When will the true Messiah come?"

Rab shook his head to clear his mind. *I have to find a way to free Jonah and Isaac,* he reminded himself, looking more carefully at the scene before him. He had watched other executions. It had been more than simple morbid curiosity; he had hoped to catch a stray Roman in an unprotected moment at best and, at worst, learn some of their tactics in case he would need the information. With that in mind he reminded himself he needed to find someone to help, so he took a closer look at the crowd.

No one here to help, he decided. *I wonder if any of Jesus' friends, or converts, or whatever they are called, are here?* he questioned. *I doubt it.*

"Move out of the way! Hey you, get back, make way," barked one of the lead soldiers as he gestured toward a small group of young men who had scurried up and were trying to find a place to watch.

It is only several hundred paces along El Wad Road from the Fort Antonio to the Benjamin Gate. This would have been an easy morning stroll for Bar-Abbas, especially since he wasn't carrying a medium sized tree truck over his shoulders and roped to his wrists. He made his way to the front of the procession hoping to catch his friend's eyes as they came by. In an endeavor unusual for him he hoped to be of some encouragement to them. But first came Jesus.

He smiled, observed Rab. *How can Jesus be smiling? He has to be in terrible pain. He is barely able to walk with that heavy beam on his shoulder and yet He smiled at that woman. There, He did it again, at that young man. What kind of man smiles on His way to be crucified?*

Not me, for sure, Rab concluded as he continued to watch Jesus interact with some of the onlookers. Just then Jesus turned his face toward Rab and looked directly at him … and smiled.

"What do you want from me?" Rab yelled out before he could stop himself. He was surprised by the words and quickly stepped back into the crowd to let Jesus and his guards pass on by. Hoping to take his mind off the embarrassing interchange he turned his attention to his friends.

Jonah seemed to be having little trouble, physically at least. Rab walked along for a while still trying to compose himself. Feeling he had, he called Jonah's name. The young thief pivoted his closest arm upward and turned his head in the direction of Rab's voice. Though they never made eye contact, Rab could tell that Jonah was still filled with fury…or fear.

After Jonah passed, Rab turned his attention to Isaac. He was limping heavily, but seemed to be managing without much assistance from the soldiers. As usual his lips were in constant motion.

Despite the difficulty and the anger he incurred by stepping on a few toes, Rab continued to watch and make his way along with the group. The closer they came to the gate the more difficult it was for all of them to negotiate through the growing crowds. Obviously some had heard the news and gathered to watch the proceedings. Others undoubtedly were travelers coming in for the festival who simply arrived at the wrong time.

Such seemed to be the case of a man from Cyrene. He happened to be close by when Jesus, now totally spent from the many wounds His body had received, fell down. It happened quickly, not that the soldiers would have tried to help if they had seen it coming. He first stumbled onto his left knee. The weight of the crossbeam caused His body to lurch to the left. The end of the beam struck the ground and before Jesus could recover, His right leg buckled. He landed on His right knee and then lunged face forward onto the dusty, stone street. With His hands tied to the crossbeam He had no way to stop His fall. The crown of thorns went flying as it smashed between His forehead and the pavement. Fresh blood shot from the new wounds made by the thorns.

The entire crowd, including Rab, gasped. In addition, the growing number of women who were now following behind began to cry aloud. They were praying or wailing so loud that few heard one of the remaining priest's reaction.

"Well I guess you aren't really a king after all, seeing that you've lost your crown."

Rab heard the comment, liked it and shouted it out himself. He was about to shout it again but caught the look of disgust in the Centurion's eyes and held his peace.

The officer called the procession to a halt, came forward and bent down to examine Jesus. He gave orders for Him to be lifted to His feet, but it was evident to all that Jesus did not have enough strength to continue under the weight of the crossbeam. The Centurion barked some orders. The soldiers untied the beam. One soldier stood it aside while the other raised Jesus to His feet.

Motioning to the nearest able-bodied man, the Centurion asked his name and his origin. When the officer was satisfied the man was from out of town and his conscription would not create a reaction from the crowd, he ordered him to pick up Jesus' crossbeam and to prepare to go with them. The soldier who had retrieved the crown of thorns put it back on Jesus' head being careful not to stick himself.

But before the march to Golgotha could continue, Jesus turned to face the distraught women. Once again they gasped as they saw His bruised and swollen face, now freshly bloody from the new wounds. With some effort Jesus held His hands up to quiet them and said, "Daughters of Jerusalem, don't cry for me. Cry for yourselves and for your children."

Rab was close enough to hear the words. If the tone had been different, he would have taken them for sarcasm, but the tone and the look of pure love in Jesus' eyes certainly communicated sincere concern. It was the same look of compassion Jesus had given him in prison and on the Rock.

What kind of person cares for others, strangers at that, when He Himself is about to die? Rab wondered.

Rab did not understand it. He shook his head to clear his mind and then he shouted, "Hey officer, don't you have some place to go with these criminals? Didn't you say, 'It is a good day to die?'"

Except for the snarl that crossed his face, the Centurion ignored Rab, but ordered his men to move the condemned men along. Simon of Cyrene was now right behind the struggling Jesus, carrying His cross. The march continued out through the Benjamin Gate.

Chapter Eighteen

The Centurion reminded his men that they could not relax just because they had gotten the execution party outside the city gate. They were only a hundred or so paces now from Golgotha and they had to keep moving.

Everyone knew the goal of Roman executions was not just to eliminate the enemies of Rome such as run-away slaves, chronic thieves, murderers, traitors, revolutionaries, and would-be deliverers, messiahs as the Jews called them. That could be done in private with a single swing of a sword. No, Rome's goal was to discourage others from even thinking about following in the footsteps of the criminals.

And the Romans designed executions to arouse more than idle curiosity. They must inspire fear, better yet, terror of Rome in as many people as possible. Therefore the condemned had to be executed in the most cruel and painful way imaginable. And the agony must be extended, lasting as long as the human body could endure it and then be relieved only by death. In addition the whole ordeal had to be carried out in a public place where the humiliation would be viewed by many, even children, whether they wanted to see it or not.

Rab figured, from a Roman's perspective, crucifixion was ideal. The Latin word meant "fixed to a cross" and as much as he hated the Romans, he knew of no better way for Rome to accomplish its goals. He also knew they weren't the only ones who used crucifixion as deterrents to crime. He had heard that the Persians had invented it. Although that nation had declined as a culture hundreds of years before, they still had the reputation of being the most heartlessly cruel people ever to walk the face of the earth.

But the Romans are not far behind, considered Rab. *Stories are rampant; the Roman Legions have crucified thousands. There are even permanent uprights outside the Esquiline Gate in the eastern wall of Rome itself. Even here outside Jerusalem they have quarried holes in the bedrock on*

Skull Hill so they don't have to dig them one at a time.

"I hate the Romans," he concluded aloud, but not loud enough to attract attention.

He also hated crucifixions. But try as he might he could think of no way to stop these that were about to happen. Rab looked up at the sky. The spring sun was bright and he thought it might be approaching the end of the first watch, around nine o'clock. His heart sank a bit lower knowing that the hotter the sun, the more agony the ordeal would bring for Jonah and Isaac ... and Jesus. A quick glance to the west gave some promise of relief as it looked like clouds were beginning to gather.

He had been thinking about the Centurion's offhanded remark that if he were a true friend, he would volunteer to take the place of his friends and be crucified in their place. Rab could honestly say he had never heard of anyone being the kind of friend that would do that. Of course there were stories of those who, in the heat of some kind of skirmish, had stepped in between a friend and an enemy and had taken a sword thrust. But certainly no one had ever done that for him, except maybe his parents, but he did not want to think about them right now. Frankly the idea of his dying in the place of Jonah and Isaac had never even entered his mind, until the Roman had said what he did.

Does anybody really do that? he wondered. *Not anybody I know, certainly not me. Not today anyway,* he concluded sadly.

It had been a while since Rab had been to Skull Hill.

"It's not the kind of place you go for recreation," he remembered telling Jonah early in their professional career together when the younger man had a natural curiosity for all things criminal or criminal related. That naturally included a place of execution of criminals.

Rab sighed as he finished his climb up the rocky embankment. He had gone on ahead of the slower group of soldiers, the men carrying crosses and the women following.

He stopped for a moment, hands on thighs, to catch his breath and to survey the area. It was not that large, about the size and height of a good-sized house. The only signs of life on the rocky surface were a few clumps of grass, struggling out of the cracks in the rock, and the constant circling of buzzards overhead. As he walked about he angrily kicked at bone fragments long since bleached by the sun.

Now in the center of Skull Hill, Rab looked for and found the three square holes that had been chiseled out of the bedrock by the Romans years ago. These were to receive and hold the crosses in place. He had forgotten that one of the holes, the center one, was on a higher terrace and behind the other two. Looking into that hole he started to say, "Well, I guess we know who will get center attention today." But then, looking once more at the other two holes he said instead, "This is not a good day to die."

Rab looked back and watched as the execution party climbed up the same path he had just taken. Jonah struggled under the weight of his cross and was being pushed by his soldier escorts. Isaac, on the other hand, had given out and one of the soldiers was carrying his crossbar. Rab watched as his old friend stumbled along grabbing at every rock outcrop available to keep himself moving.

The man carrying Jesus' cross was having little trouble. The two soldiers with Jesus had joined Him on both sides and were all but dragging Him up the incline. From the look on their faces, they were not too happy about getting close enough to Him to get His blood on their uniforms. His robe was soaked and the crown of thorns was almost a weapon in itself.

Or at least it could be if He knew how to use it, Rab observed derisively.

There was not a lot of room in front of the places where the crosses would stand and the lead soldiers soon set up a perimeter to keep that portion of the hill clear for them to work. Rab moved away without having to be prodded and the portion of the crowd who had decided to climb the hill stayed to the back and sides of the area. The women and most of the onlookers had begun to line the road down below. Suddenly, some of them had to scurry out of the way as a wagon pulled by two black horses arrived. It displayed the Roman eagle emblem and was driven by two soldiers. These and two others who were riding in the back immediately jumped out and began to carry the cross standards up Skull Hill.

Rab noticed that the only others who were allowed in the main work area were several priests and other leaders of the Sanhedrin, the Jewish court, and he wondered why they were here.

Since the Romans are doing their dirty work for them, Rab conjectured. *I guess they are here to make sure it is done correctly; or maybe they are here to make sure the would-be messiah is finished. Maybe, like most politicians they want to be at the center of attention. Maybe despite their holier than thou attitude, they just like blood.*

Rab decided he didn't know and didn't care. He was suddenly very weary. He sat down on a small patch of grass, leaned up against a rock and rubbed his temples as he continued to watch what he feared might be a life-altering event.

Chapter Nineteen

Jonah and Isaac were forced to watch the crucifixion of Jesus. Rab and the rest of the crowd watched too. The soldiers took one of the cross standards and laid it on the ground just above the center hole. Then they took the crossbeam from the Cyrene, and attached it firmly with ropes to the standard. Next they stripped Jesus' robe and undergarments from Him and pushed Him toward His cross. They made Him sit on it. The two positioned themselves, one at Jesus' feet and the other at His left side. The rest of the operation seemed to fall to the soldiers who had arrived in the wagon. One of them produced a jug and poured some liquid onto a sponge and offered it to Jesus.

A priest who was watching asked the Centurion about the drink. The officer told him it was wine mixed with myrrh, a painkiller. He added in all seriousness, "We have coined a word for the horrific pain these men will experience. The word is "excruciating" and it means "from the cross." There is no other pain like what they will feel when the nails are driven into their hands. The nails pierce through a nerve that runs between the bones in their forearms. The pain feels like fire and it rips through the entire body. Once the nails are in place every little movement creates a new flame of fire. I know they are criminals, but I have ordered my men to give them some relief. It is not much, but it will help them through this part."

The priest just shrugged his shoulders.

When Jesus tasted the wine, He refused to drink it, turning His face to the side. The Centurion walked over to Him and, though his words could not be heard, it appeared to Rab that he was trying to convince Jesus to take the drug. Jesus looked calmly at the officer but must have continued to refuse the drink. Finally, the officer turned, gestured to his men and walked back over to the priests.

Rab could not hear the explanation, but whatever it

was it must not have made sense because all of them, including the Roman, shook their heads.

It puzzled Rab too. *What kind of man refuses to take a painkiller when He is about to have spikes driven through His hands and feet?* He had to admit, a lot about this would-be, but soon-to-be-dead, messiah puzzled him.

With the wine put away and the original two guards in position, the soldiers from the wagon continued with their duties. They shoved Jesus' shredded back onto the course wood of the upright and stretched out His hands. His back began to bleed again. While one man pulled Jesus' right hand tight against the crossbeam, the second soldier placed His boot on Jesus' left arm. The third man straddled Jesus, sitting on His chest, His hands free to help however needed. The fourth soldier appeared to hide what he was doing from Jesus but not from the onlookers.

Rab looked over at Isaac and Jonah. Isaac had an anguished look on his face. His two guards had their hands securely on His neck to keep him still. But they could not keep him from praying. Jonah's face was harder to read. Rab knew he was glad to see Jesus die, but the fact that he would shortly suffer the same fate killed any thoughts of rejoicing.

The soldier produced a metal spike that appeared to Rab to be as thick as his thumb on one end, sharp on the other and as long as his hand. The soldier knelt below the outstretched hand of Jesus' right hand, placed the point of the spike between Jesus' wrist bones and drew back the hammer.

Jesus's eyes jerked wide open, His head moving back and forth.

Was He saying, 'No!' or searching the heavens for help? Rab wondered.

The scream everyone expected did not come. In its place, from somewhere deep within him came one word.

"FATHER ..."

The metallic ring of metal on metal sounded again.

"FATHER ..."

And again.

"FATHER …"

Following each hammer blow, Jesus cried out.

Shortly, the soldier with the hammer and nails moved to Jesus' left side. The other soldiers shifted as well. The hammer rang out again.

Again Jesus cried out.

"FATHER …"

But this time His eyes no longer searched the heavens, but rather the faces of each of the soldiers around him.

Ring!!!

"FATHER … FORGIVE THEM…"

Ring!!!

"FOR THEY…"

The soldiers now looked back at Him, into His eyes and He into theirs.

Ring!!!

"DON'T KNOW…"

Now Jesus was looking at those who were standing nearby: Isaac, Jonah, the priests, the Centurion …

Ring!!!

"WHAT THEY…"

Jesus' gaze broadened. His eyes searched out … and caught … Rab's.

Ring!!!

"DO!!!"

Chapter Twenty

"Father, forgive them for they don't know what they do."

Jesus continued to catch and look deeply into the eyes of those around Him even as the soldiers continued their gruesome work. They bent His legs and placed them on each side of the upright. They nailed a spike through His left heel, then His right. Satisfied that Jesus was secured, they nailed the announcement that Pilate had ordered to the top of His cross. Finally, with all six soldiers joining in they raised His cross up and then dropped it in the hole.

The soldiers made little attempt to slow the cross as it dropped into the hole. As the cross hit the bottom of the hole, the full weight of Jesus' body now pulled at the four nails, multiplying the agony. He was supported now only by the nails in His hands and feet and the ropes securing His forearms. He now began a constant struggle to breathe. There was no position He found that brought relief from the tremendous pain now racing like white heat through His arms and legs. The wounds on his back were ripped open again and every movement brought rough wood into contact with raw nerves.

The soldiers now turned their attention to Jonah who had been cursing through the entire ordeal with Jesus. The young thief had stopped only briefly when his eyes met Jesus'. When he realized Jesus was praying for him Jonah started cursing again. Blows to his mouth from his two guards only had caused him to change the object of his rant from Jesus to them. Now the wagon soldiers joined with the others to get him "up on the tree" and quiet as quickly as possible. Rather than decline the wine myrrh mixture, Jonah was still squeezing and sucking the sponge when they pried it from his hands.

Rab watched helplessly as the soldiers stripped Jonah of his garments, pushed him down and began the process of crucifying his young friend. The old thief had never been married. He may have some children out there somewhere, the product of his infrequent interaction with prostitutes, but if so, he was not aware of them. Jonah was the closest he would probably ever come to having a son and now he was being tortured and killed in front of Rab's very eyes.

So many feelings flooded Rab's heart he could not sort them out: hatred for the Romans, contempt for the priests, remorse for his role in shaping Jonah's life, guilt that he was free and his friends were dying. The notion of offering himself as a substitute again surfaced in Rab's mind, fueled by Jonah's now constant screams of agony.

"That is stupid," he decided, and to add emphasis, declared just above a whisper. "Jonah made his own choices. Sure I led in some, but I never forced him. He is still responsible."

The rationalizations did not mollify him at all. In fact, the depth of his own sorrow only increased as Jonah's cross was lifted and Rab could see the young man writhing in tremendous pain. With his cross secured in place in front of and to Jesus' left, Jonah focused on breathing. Rab looked away as the soldiers turned to crucify Isaac.

Shortly, despite the wine and myrrh painkiller, Isaac too was screaming with every strike of the hammer. Instead of cursing the soldiers, however, he was praying to the top of his lungs.

"God, help me! God, help me! Oh God, it hurts. Help me!"

Once his cross was standing upright and secured in place just to the front and to Jesus' right, he too became quieter, but not still.

All three crucified men were now in constant motion: up and down, up and down, up and down.

Rab recalled heated discussions he'd had regarding crucifixion. Few agreed on the origin of the depravity that would motivate men to act in such harsh ways toward other men, even criminals. Some thought it Satanic, some demonic, some that the cruelty was mined from the darkest depths of the human soul. All agreed that crucifixion was evil and genius. It pitted three of man's strongest needs against each other: the need to breathe against the need to avoid pain all in the context of the need to just simply stay alive.

Hanging by his arms, a man's chest muscles are stretched and do not function properly. In that position he can breathe in but not out. In order to exhale he must be able to relax his chest. That requires him to push up with his legs while pulling up with his arms. Because all of his weight is on the nails in his hands and feet the pain quickly becomes unbearable. Normally a strong man could hold himself up for quite a while, but not in this case. After only a brief time, the man must relax and let his body slump once more. Of course that put him back in the first position from which he cannot breathe. So the process is repeated, then again, and again.

Now Rab watched as this most brutal mode of execution was displayed before him. Isaac, Jonah ... and Jesus were still trying to develop their own rhythms in their work to stay alive. That all three were in such agony was obvious as each man pulled up to exhale and held himself as long as he could. When the pain became unbearable each would get a breath and let himself down. As lungs began to burn from the need to breathe out, each would push up again, creating more pain resulting in another slump. And so the cycle continued: up, down, up, down.

As their muscles tire and their desire to live wanes, this grotesque dance, if you can call it that, will be constantly changing, thought Rab, *but they will go on for a very long time. As long as they can pull and push themselves up they will breathe ... and they will live.*

Crucifixion is not a quiet ordeal, Rab also noticed as all three were working. The grunts and groans from their labor were often interrupted by outbursts of pain – as if one were touched by a hot iron repeatedly and at random.

A new idea slowly formed in Rab's mind. He became aware that each man was expressing his agony in a different way. While all were limited to the brief bits of time they were up and exhaling, Isaac's outbursts continued to be mixed with prayers for help. Jonah always cursed.

Someone said that a man dies the same way he lived. That sure seems to be true with Isaac and Jonah.

I wonder if when I die it will reveal how I lived?" the thoughts kept coming. *"How have I lived?*

He then caught himself looking at, watching Jesus. Despite his hatred for the man Rab had to admit that His dying contrasted both to Jonah's bitterness and Isaac's desperation.

He is in pain alright, but look at Him. What is that? A calmness? Peace? I don't get it. What's going on? questioned Rab.

Not liking the implications of his thoughts he closed his eyes, but instead of relief, the picture of Jesus' eyes looking deeply into his in the prison formed in his mind. He jerked his eyes open to erase that image only to see that Jesus, in spite of his agony, was even now looking directly at him.

Those eyes …!

Rab could not bear to look into those eyes and so he once again closed his eyes and leaned back.

Chapter Twenty-one

Rab was suddenly very weary. He could barely think, much less try to determine if his fatigue was due to lack of sleep or to his darkening mood. He felt helpless and hopeless. He did not want to watch the agony of his friends on their crosses, but neither did he want to abandon them. For a while he considered taking a nap.

To clear his head he slapped himself in the face, stood up, twisted his shoulders and moved his head from side to side. Looking up at the sun, which was now obstructed by a thickening layer of clouds, he estimated it must be approaching noon. He forced himself to look once again toward the crosses.

The wagon soldiers were now finished with their duties. After some words with and a salute to the Centurion, they gathered up their tools and left. The officer released another four soldiers who went back down the hill.

Probably back to the barracks to await their watch, concluded Rab. He continued to observe as two soldiers stood watch while the remaining four set up a camp of sorts behind and to the side of the crosses. They weren't too far from where Rab was still sitting. It appeared that the soldiers would rotate in pairs guarding the crucified to make sure they were not taken down pre-maturely. From time to time, a soldier offered drinks of the wine myrrh. Isaac and Jonah always accepted; Jesus never did.

The off-duty soldiers then began to divide among themselves the confiscated garments of the condemned.

"They won't need these anymore," one said holding up some of the garments and jerking his head in the direction of the crucified.

What started out as a simple exercise suddenly turned into an argument over who should get what. One soldier became so frustrated that he suddenly tore Jesus' outer garment into four pieces and handed a part to each of his three comrades.

"You didn't have to do that," a second said, looking at the piece of torn cloth in his hands. "What am I supposed to do with this?" A third soldier was nodding his head in agreement.

"I'll tell you what you can do with it," retorted the first as he moved angrily toward the second.

"Wait a minute," said the fourth soldier. He had stayed out of the argument and was now holding up Jesus' blood soaked inner garment. "We don't want to tear this up. It's all one piece."

The other three soldiers stopped, looked at Him, then at the cloth and then back to the soldier holding it.

One finally spoke, "I thought you were a little strange. Have a thing for undergarments do you?"

The laughter that followed sounded completely out of place, even if a portion of it was a desire to relieve the tension. Nonetheless it attracted the attention of the Centurion who turned and walked quickly toward the soldiers.

"What's going on over here?" the officer demanded.

The four men immediately came to attention, holding the various pieces of clothing to their sides.

"Sir, we were just dividing up the thieves' garments when the under..., uh, clothing expert here suggested we keep the King's inner garment in one piece.

The Centurion looked at the soldier who had Jesus' undergarment. He held it up for the officer to see.

"Sir, I have never seen anything like this. I don't know how they made this. It is woven into one piece and doesn't have any seams."

"Let me have that," the Centurion demanded.

"Yes sir! I'm sorry sir," he said handing the bloodied garment to the officer.

"It's not stitched together like the others, and I ..."

The soldier abruptly stopped his explanation when he saw that the Centurion was now looking past the garment to the man to whom it belonged.

"Why is it that everything about that man is so different?" the officer questioned, more to himself than to his men. For a long while he continued to look from Jesus to the garment and back.

"Sir? Sir? What do you want us to do with it?"

"Do whatever you like," the officer finally replied. "Just do it in an orderly manner," he said, taking one final look at the garment then handing it back to the soldier. Without another word he walked toward the group of priests.

The soldiers relaxed. They passed the garment around and finally agreed it was unique. They also agreed it might be of value. After some discussion they decided to cast lots to see who would become its new owner.

Chapter Twenty-two

When the Centurion got back to the group of priests he was greeted by Joseph Caiaphas, the Jewish High Priest. Despite his extra broad smile and lavish compliments on a "well executed execution," the officer could tell from the tone of his voice that the religious leader of the Jewish people was upset about something. Caiaphas requested a private audience; so the rest of the priests excused themselves and moved a short distance away.

With his eyes locked onto those of the Centurion, Caiaphas pointed toward Jesus' cross and asked, "What is the meaning of that?"

"What, your Excellency?" the Centurion asked as he turned to look in the direction the priest was pointing.

"That sign. It is inaccurate and it is a disgrace. It has to be changed or taken down."

The Centurion took a couple of steps toward the center cross and looked intently at the sign his men had placed above the head of Jesus. Written in Hebrew, Latin and Greek were the words,

"JESUS THE NAZARENE,
THE KING OF THE JEWS."

"It looks alright to me," said the officer, still looking at the sign, "What is the problem?"

"The problem is that it is wrong. This man is not 'The King of the Jews.' That sign should say, 'He said he was the King of the Jews.' or 'He claimed to be King of the Jews'"

The Centurion, with the priest on his heels, walked up to Jesus' cross and looked up at the sign. After studying it again, he looked more intently at Jesus. For an instant the two men's eyes met. Despite the agony of Jesus' ordeal, it was the Centurion who broke the contact, shrugged and turned to study the face of Caiaphas.

What a contrast, he thought to himself. But what he

said was, "Take it up with the Governor; those are his words, not mine."

The officer then turned and walked back to where his soldiers were resting.

The High Priest stared at the Centurion's back, the nap of his own neck turning red. The rest of the priests quickly gathered around him. He dispatched two of them to Pilate to lodge a formal complaint about the sign and to seek to have it changed. As the two left, the rest turned and watched Jesus labor in silence on the cross. After a long time Caiaphas finally spoke, loudly enough for everyone around to hear.

"He saved others; He cannot save Himself. If He is the King of Israel; let Him come down from the cross and we will believe in Him."

A second priest, recalling one of the main accusations against Jesus at the trial suddenly shouted at Him, "You who are going to destroy the temple and rebuild it in three days, save yourself! If you are the Son of God, come down from the cross."

In response another priest began to chant, quietly at first, "Come down! Come down! Come down!"

Soon the other priests and religious leaders joined in, "Come down! Come down! Come down!"

Others who had been watching from afar, emboldened by the priest's derision of Jesus, drew closer, wagged their heads at Him and joined the mockery.

Someone shouted above the den, "He trusts in God; let God rescue Him now, if He delights in Him for He said, 'I am the Son of God'"

The Centurion, upon hearing the growing commotion ordered the two soldiers who were preparing to relieve the first two men to hurry and take up positions beside them. But the two off- duty soldiers left the lunches they were preparing and joined in the ridicule. They brought their wine with them and raised a toast to Jesus daring Him by saying, "If you are the King of the Jews, save yourself!"

Jonah, stirred from his mindless labor, was grateful for the diversion from his own suffering. He turned his head as far as he could to the right toward Jesus and with each pull and push up he ranted, "Are you the Messiah or not? ... If you are, save yourself ... and us!"

Isaac had also been roused and had been trying to understand the uproar. When he heard what Jonah said he shifted to his left as far as he could and shouted at him.

"You need to shut up! ... Don't you fear God at all? ... You are about to die! ... And we deserve what we are getting ... but He doesn't ... He didn't do anything wrong ... He is innocent!"

The Centurion had stationed himself directly in front of the crucified and had been watching and listening to all that had taken place. Rab, roused from his weariness by the angry shouts of the crowd, decided to join in as they made sport of Jesus. But as he was making his way to the center of the mob he went past the Centurion and for a brief moment, caught the officer's disapproving eye, so he simply listened to the exchanges.

Now as the two men stood looking up into the bruised, blooded and tear-stained face of Jesus, neither could avoid the depth of concern in Jesus' eyes. One, then the other had to avert his eyes. Looking beyond Jesus now both noticed the sky. It had become as dark, foreboding and pervasive as the cruelty they were watching.

"I have never seen clouds so dark," Rab muttered.

"And angry," the Centurion agreed. "It's as if they are trying to extinguish the light of the sun."

Suddenly, the black boiling clouds completed their assault on the sun and Skull Hill became as dark as night. The sudden darkness caused a hush to descend on the crowd; the railing against Jesus stopped. Sounds of the relentless toil of the three men on the cross could still be heard, but even Jonah ceased his cursing.

Isaac, however, responded differently. Despite the pain he struggled to pull and push up, turning his head as far to his left as he could. Straining with all his might he finally got enough breath to cry out, "Jesus ... remember me ... when you enter ... your kingdom."

Jesus pulled and pushed himself up and, looking over to Isaac, spoke softly but firmly.

"I tell you the truth ... today ... you will join me ... in paradise."

Chapter Twenty-three

The Centurion immediately barked orders to his men for them to light torches. Because they were not prepared, and it was as dark as night, the chore took longer than usual. Meanwhile the darkness had a chilling effect on the mockers. They quickly gathered into smaller groups and moved away. Rab decided to go back to his seat. First he touched Jonah's leg, but no words of comfort came to his mind. He then walked past Isaac and spoke briefly to him. Both friends were in such pain that neither acknowledged his presence.

Even with the light of the soldiers' torches it was difficult to see, but with the crowd thinned out, Rab had just sat down when he noticed a small group of women approaching the crosses. One of the women was being assisted by a man, his uncovered face a contrast to the covered heads of the women. The small cluster stopped directly in front of Jesus, their whispers barely audible amidst their sobs.

Besides the usual people of compassion in every crowd, Rab thought it curious that none of Jesus' family or followers had come forward to comfort or support Him. He wondered why. Maybe they were just now learning this was happening. Maybe they were embarrassed to be associated with a condemned man. Maybe they were afraid they themselves would become targets of abuse or even violence. Maybe they had been here all along, but had just now gained courage from the darkness and the dispersal of the crowds.

One of the women took off her shawl and handed it to the man. She whispered something to him. He nodded, took the shawl and, with some difficulty wrapped it around Jesus' thighs. After tying it in place he stepped back to the woman. The group stayed close to Jesus for some time, looking up into His face, speaking to Him, gently caressing His feet and legs. For His part, Jesus seemed to be aware of their presence, but if He spoke, Rab could not hear. From time to time the women exchanged positions taking turns, it seemed attending to Him. It was during one of those times that Rab was startled because he thought he recognized one of the women.

No, it couldn't be, he puzzled. *The light is not good. I must be mistaken.*

But now his curiosity had been peaked, so Rab slowly and quietly moved closer to get a better look, being careful to stay outside the light from the torches. Again the women traded places and to his utter astonishment he became certain he recognized one of them. He could not recall her name but was sure their paths had crossed even if he could not say where or when.

The older woman, with the help of the man who now appeared to be about Jonah's age, was standing in front of and below Jesus. Her words to him were gentle and consoling, but except for the use of His name, Rab could not understand what she was saying. Then he heard her call Him Son.

Son? She's His mother! The idea startled Rab.

From deep inside his gut, a dark and ugly feeling began to awaken. Numbed by the suffering of his friends, Rab had forgotten his own frustration and hatred. Now it was stirring. Rab wanted to revel in the familiarity of the emotion. He was tempted to shout that the fake savior was getting what He deserved, but he stifled the words if not a wicked smile. He continued to watch the scene in front of him, eerie in the torchlight, particularly the woman and Jesus.

One of the other women, the one Rab thought he recognized, was now steadying the Mother on one side while the young man supported her on the other. Jesus took a painful breath, drew Himself up and with a raspy voice barely louder than a whisper spoke to His mother.

"Woman, behold your son."

He sunk down once more, took another breath, pulled up again and said to the man.

"Behold your mother!"

Rab watched as the young man put an arm around the woman. In turn she rested her head on his shoulder. Her weeping was audible. Jesus continued His struggle to breathe.

Rab was conflicted, his tired mind a cacophony of thoughts.

How can He do that? What kind of man does that, looking out for others while dying on a cross? Well, it is his mother. At least he has a mother. If it weren't for him I might have known my mother...and father. He deserves to die. Again he wanted to scream out, *Serves you right!*

With eyes on fire, he glared up at Jesus. To Rab's amazement, in spite of the fact that he was standing in the shadows, it appeared that Jesus was again focused completely on him. Rab did not even try to "stare down" those eyes. He simply stepped back, turned and stumbled back over to his place by the rock. He sat down and no sooner had his back hit the rock than he was asleep.

The shouting startled Rab. As he opened his eyes he thought it was the middle of the night. Turning in the direction of the noise he recalled, with some difficulty, his setting. There were the torches, the soldiers now on alert, and a host of others, priests included, who were pointing and shouting.

You idiot, you must have fallen asleep, Rab chastised himself as he summoned all his energy to urge his brain and body to become fully awake. He looked up to the sun to see how long he had slept. The dark cloud cover was still in place but the middle of the western sky was a fraction lighter than the rest. From it Rab determined it to be around midafternoon. He stood up, shook his legs and circled around behind those making all the commotion.

As he drew near he saw one of the onlookers point to Jesus and say, "This man is calling for Elijah."

"Let's see if Elijah will come to save Him," one responded.

"Yeah, let's see," said another with a sneer.

One of the priests held his hands up, quieting the crowd and said, "No! He's not calling for Prophet Elijah. Don't you remember your studies? The messiah here is quoting the Psalmist, What he said was, 'My God, my God, why have You forsaken me?'"

One of the other priests said, "I can quote that Psalm too," and turning toward Jesus he shouted,
>Commit yourself to the LORD;
>let Him deliver Him;
>Let Him rescue Him,
>because He delights in Him.

"If the LORD delights in Him, He will rescue Him, right?" he continued.

"Of course," they all agreed, laughing among themselves.

Rab noticed that the soldiers were once again on alert. He looked around for the Centurion and was startled to see that the officer had moved up behind him, not more than an arm's length away. He was watching, as was Rab, from the shadows.

Just then another priest spoke up, "I remember some of that Psalm too. We had to memorize it in school. The verses that stuck with me are,
>"I am poured out like water,
>And all my bones are out of joint;
>My heart is like wax;
>It is melted within me.
>My strength is dried up like a potsherd,
>And my tongue cleaves to my jaws…"

His recitation and the crowd's derision was cut short when Jesus suddenly cried out, "I am thirsty."

A man Rab had not seen before, stepped out of the shadows and walked to the jar the soldiers had placed below the crosses. He took the sponge, dipped it in the sour wine, placed it on a hyssop reed and lifted up to Jesus.

Jesus wet His lips and cleared His throat. Then, it seemed, with all His might, pushed Himself up and as He surveyed the entire group of onlookers, spoke quietly but emphatically.

"It is finished!"

The silence was as deep as the darkness.

Once again Jesus cleared His throat. This time He looked up to the blackened sky and shouted.

"Father, into your hands I commit my spirit."

His body then relaxed and his head slumped on His chest.

Almost instantly the silence was broken by the sound of a ram's horn coming from a distance behind them.

"What is that?" one of the men in the group asked quietly?

"That is the Temple trumpet," explained one of the priests absently. "It is announcing the completion of the sacrifice of the Passover lambs."

Suddenly the ground began to shake violently. Those who were not knocked to the ground quickly lay down and grabbed whatever they could to steady themselves. Several large rocks split in two while others broke loose and went tumbling down the hill toward the road. Everyone below scrambled for safety away from the hill and the falling rocks. Rab had never felt anything so violent in all his life.

The shaking stopped as quickly as it had begun. The dark clouds, as if loosened by the quake, also began to break up. Before long the afternoon sun was once again shining bright.

The Centurion, who had been knocked down, was now on his feet and moving to take his position with his soldiers in front of the crosses. First he studied the condemned to make sure they were still secure. Then he looked at the sky, the broken rocks and the groups of men still lying on the ground. All of his soldiers, even those who had been resting, took defensive positions around him as if they, though obviously fearful, could defend their leader against the violence of nature.

Gaining his composure the Centurion gave his men the order to stand at ease. Once again he turned to study Jesus. Slowly at first and then with vigor he began to shake his head back and forth. The moment was not lost on his soldiers. They remained quiet until one could stand it no longer.

He blurted out, "Sir, have we done something wrong? I mean … the earthquake and …"

"That weird darkness!" another soldier interrupted. "What does it all mean?"

For a long time the Centurion continued to stare at the now still body of Jesus. Finally he asked, "Did you see the way He died?"

Pivoting slowly he studied the faces of each of his men, as if seeing them for the first time. Then he turned around toward the crowd. He had the attention of every single person on Skull Hill. When his eyes met Rab's there was a slight flicker of recognition.

Finally the Centurion spoke clearly and loudly enough for all to hear.

"This was an innocent man."

When the amazed onlookers said nothing in response, the officer spoke again, "I tell you, truly this was the Son of God!"

Chapter Twenty-four

The words could have had no greater impact if they had been spoken by the High Priest himself. They registered instantly on everyone who heard them. Like the rest, Rab looked up at the now still body of Jesus, crown of thorns and all. Next he stared at the sign above his head, "Jesus the Nazarene The King of the Jews!" Thoughts of his first encounter with Jesus in the prison in Caiaphas' house came back to him.

Those eyes ...

He was grateful that those eyes were now closed. As he looked around it was obvious the Centurion's words had struck home. Others tore their eyes away from the crucified man in front of them. Some looked up toward the heavens first, but all eventually looked down. No one else spoke, but one and then another turned and with the traditional sign of grief, beat their chests as they slipped away.

Rab did not feel remorse. What he felt was confusion.

This is not the way this is supposed to end! he wanted to say to someone, anyone or everyone. But they were all gone, all except the soldiers and the priests. He looked again at the crosses. The only two friends he had in the world were still hanging there. They were still in pain and they were still struggling. He then remembered Isaac's words to Jonah, "We are getting what we deserve. Jesus is innocent."

Could that be true? Was Jesus innocent?

He was shaken by the direction his thoughts were going and he refused to follow that path.

"No, no, no!" he said out loud.

The words of Jesus to Isaac came to mind, "Today you will be with me in Paradise."

Today ... today? Paradise? Rab was not sure what Paradise meant, so he focused on the word, *Today*.

He recalled that it usually takes at least two days, maybe as many as four for men to die of crucifixion, depending on their strength and how much support they have for their feet. He looked again at Isaac and Jonah. Both were still in great pain and struggling up and down. The older man's cycles were definitely slower than Jonah's but he appeared to Rab to be a long way from giving up. Covering his eyes he glanced at the sun and saw that it was getting low in the sky, maybe two hours before sunset.

You messed up preacher! Rab wanted to shout. *You may have died early, maybe because of the blood loss, but Isaac here is going to make it past sundown and that means it will be tomorrow, not today when he dies. You are a faker for sure,* he concluded, *nothing innocent about you!*

His thoughts were interrupted by an argument that had erupted between the priests and the Centurion. He heard the priests instructing the Roman to take the men down from the cross. Rab could hardly believe what he was hearing. He stepped closer. Sure enough, the priests were reminding the officer that the coming Sabbath (at sunset) was also part of the Passover Feast and was therefore a "high Sabbath" or special holy day. If the men were still on the crosses, they would spoil the occasion. They had to come down, now.

For a moment it sounded to Rab as if the priests were concerned about his two friends and they wanted the soldiers to stop the executions. His heart beat faster as he thought that Isaac and Jonah might be spared. He knew that stopping a crucifixion was rare, but not totally unheard of. He remembered a story of three men who were taken down from their crosses. Two died anyway but the third actually lived, though maimed for life.

But at least he had a life, concluded Rab.

Then he heard one of the priests say, "I don't care whether they live or die. Just get them down."

The rage of years of disappointment at the religious leaders of his nation instantly hit the boiling point. It was all he could do to hold in his venom. He felt that religion only kept people in bondage. Laws and rules only point out where people fail. These priests did not care about people. They only cared about their positions and the power they held. *It's okay to kill someone on Friday but not Saturday.*

His thoughts were interrupted by the Centurion who retorted, "I have my orders, but nonetheless, I think we can accommodate you. If you make a formal request to the Governor, I am sure he will issue the order. I will send a couple of my soldiers to accompany you."

Rab watched as the officer called two of the soldiers to himself and spoke to them. One of the priests also gave instructions to a couple of others who immediately turned and started down the hill behind the soldiers. The only words he could hear were those called out after the two, "If you need help with the Governor, go see the High Priest."

Rab noticed another man, dressed in a very nice robe, who must have been listening, for he also turned and followed after the priests.

Is that the man who gave the drink to Jesus when he cried out? Rab wondered.

Time moved as slowly as the sun seeking its rest in the western horizon. Rab sat back down and watched the shadows around him reach out to the east. He did not know what else to do. He really wanted to just get up and leave, like the rest of the crowd, or most of it anyway. He did notice that the group of women and that young man were still watching from a distance. A couple of priests were also seated on the ground, seeming to enjoy their conversation.

They probably are here to make sure Jesus stays dead, Rab thought absently and then wondered where that strange idea came from. Isaac and Jonah were still on their crosses. Jonah's curses mixed with Isaac's prayers were the only normal part of this bizarre experience.

I'm not doing anybody any good. Maybe I should just leave, get away from here,
Rab turned the idea over in his mind. *Where can I go? I can't stay here in Jerusalem or at least if I do, I can't keep stealing*

or killing Roman soldiers. Everybody knows me now. What can I do?

Rab became morose as he considered the fact that he really didn't have much to live for and never had really, except his desire to live up to his name, Joshua, the deliverer. Now he resigned himself to the reality that he couldn't deliver anyone from anything - not his country from the Romans and not Isaac and Jonah from death. Rab stopped himself.

What a selfish bum! Here you are thinking about yourself ... feeling sorry for yourself ... while your best friends are not ten paces away, dying on crosses. Maybe that's what I ought to do ... no, not the cross ... just some other way.

Rab looked over at the crosses and considered the Romans. There were only two still standing watch and now only two others resting.

The officer makes five, he calculated. *That's pretty good odds. I probably could take one or two with me, maybe the resting ones, before they got me.*

What little bit of energy this inner debate had generated in Rab suddenly drained when he saw the two soldiers and priests who had gone into the city now coming back up the hill. Following behind was the man in the expensive robe. After shrugging off his disappointment, or was it relief, he stood up and walked over to see if they were going to take Isaac and Jonah down from their crosses.

"Here are your orders," one of the priests said, handing the Centurion a small parchment. The Centurion read the document, noted the seal on it and gave an order to the two soldiers who had just returned. They turned and walked toward the crosses. It was then Rab noticed that one carried a large wooden club that had been concealed behind his right leg.

"Nooooo!" Rab bellowed as he lunged in the direction of the soldier with the club. Both soldiers immediately turned to face him, one drawing his sword, the other lifting the club.

In the same instant the Centurion shouted a command as he also turned to counter the attack. Before Rab could even draw the small dagger he always carried, the man with the club hit him across his left thigh just above the knee. The force knocked him to the ground, face down in agony. When he tried to get up on his knees the pain was so sharp that he hesitated. In that moment, one of the soldiers kicked him over on his back. Before he could react, both of the remaining two soldiers had their spearheads pointed inches above his neck.

The Centurion stepped in beside the soldiers, looked down at Rab and asked, "Have you changed your mind? Are you ready to die in place of your friends?" Then he added, "or do you just wish to die with them?"

Rab's only response was to scowl at him so the officer told the two with the spears to keep the thief away from the crosses. He then said to the soldier with the club, "You have your orders, break their legs."

Rab could not watch. He rolled over on his face, slowly got up on his knees and with much pain, began crawling away. He winced at the sound of wood smashing into bone and Jonah's immediate scream of agony made possible only because he had kicked upward with his remaining good leg. Again Rab recoiled at the sound of bone being crushed, but this time there was no scream. Rab knew that with both shin bones broken, Jonah would be able to breathe only as long as he could pull up with his arms. The fact that he did not scream or curse meant that his arms were spent. Death was minutes away. Rab crawled a bit further away then lay on the ground. He placed his hands over his ears so that he would not have to hear the sounds of Isaac's legs being crushed.

Rab had lain on the ground until his fury and shame were spent. He painfully rolled over on his back, sat up and looked around. Jonah and Isaac were not moving, their heads slumped down on their chests. Shattered shinbones punched through their skin at grotesque angles. The soldiers were carrying their ladder toward Jonah's cross, preparing to remove his body. To keep from throwing up, Rab focused on the man who was talking to the Centurion.

"Sir, please let me introduce myself. My name is Joseph and I am a member of the Jewish High Court. I have been a follower of Jesus of Nazareth for a while, a disciple, a secret one I am ashamed to say. I did not agree with His death, but I do agree with your assessment, 'He was an innocent man.' I also believed, as you said, 'He was the Son of God.'"

The man looked at a piece of parchment he held in his hands and then offered it to the officer. "I have been given permission from the Governor to take His body, once you have verified to him that He is dead."

The Centurion studied the document and then walked over and stood beneath the still body of Jesus. He glanced at the priests who were watching carefully. Then he ordered one of the soldiers to bring his spear and thrust it into Jesus' side. Rab observed as the soldier placed his spear tip under the clearly visible lowest rib of Jesus' right side. With one motion he thrust it violently upward. There was no reaction from Jesus, but the soldier jumped back as water and then blood gushed out of the wound.

"I have my proof," said the Centurion. "I will report his death to the Governor and then you can have His body." After issuing orders, the officer took two of his men and left Skull Hill.

While the remaining soldiers began to take Isaac and Jonah down from their crosses, Rab watched and, for the first time, wondered where his friends would be buried. The rich man was gathering the group of women and, Rab noticed, a few men around him to prepare to remove Jesus from the cross. It looked to Rab as if they were going to do so with the utmost of care. The opposite was happening with his friends. One of the soldiers placed his ladder against the crossbar behind Jonah's left hand. He climbed up, loosened the rope and slid it up toward his body, then using the handle of his hammer, roughly pried loose Jonah's hand from the spike. As the arm came loose, his body slumped grotesquely to the side suspended only by the rope. The soldier then moved the ladder to the other side and repeated the actions. Another soldier had been prying Jonah's feet loose. Jonah's body was now being suspended only by the ropes holding his arms to the crossbeam.

Rab watched in horror as the soldier on the ladder drew his sword and began to slash at the remaining ropes. Rab rushed forward shouting at the soldier to be more careful. The soldier looked at him as if to say, *Who cares? They are only thieves, and dead thieves at that.* When Rab softened his voice from commanding to pleading, then to begging, the soldier shrugged and motioned to the men on the ground. One of them picked up a length of rope and threw it up to him. He wrapped it over the crossbeam, under the arms and around Jonah's body. He then cut the ropes and with the men on the ground holding the long rope, lowered the thief's body to the ground. Rab rushed in to drag the body clear.

The soldier repositioned his ladder against the upright and began to untie the ropes holding the crossbar. Another soldier hollered up at him, "It's going to be dark soon, why don't you leave that for latter?" The soldier on the ladder shrugged his shoulder and climbed down.

Following the same procedure, they took down Isaac's body. Once again Rab moved in to drag the corpse away. He laid it beside that of Jonah and collapsed. He did not feel like doing any more and was just going to sit there. However the crowd around Jesus' cross got his attention. The priests had drawn to one side and were all but shouting at each other.

"What do you mean, the veil of temple has ripped in two?" one of them demanded. He was looking at a young man who obviously had just arrived with the news.

"Sir, I am only telling you what His Excellency Caiaphas told me to tell you," he replied.

"But that is very sturdy cloth and it is thicker than a man's hand. How could it have ripped?" the priest wanted to know.

"I don't know sir, but it did…and from the top to the bottom," the messenger concluded.

The angst on the faces of the priests was evident. They obviously wanted to go to the Temple but their business here was not concluded until they could guarantee that Jesus was truly dead.

The Centurion returned and began watching as the rich man, the women and several others took Jesus' body down. Rab was struck by how tender they were and even that the soldiers allowed them the use of their ladders and tools. They used a linen cloth instead of ropes to lower the body. With the body down, the rich man wrapped Jesus carefully in the cloth. He and another man carried Jesus' body away, the rest of the group following quietly behind. The last of the onlookers also wandered away. Soon the soldiers had their equipment packed and they left Skull Hill as well.

Despite himself, Rab began to tense as the soldier tapped another on the arm and both turned and started toward Rab and his two dead friends.

"You need to move on now so we can finish our job," the first soldier said to Rab.

"What do you mean?" Rab asked, trying to remain calm.

"We have to take these two and give them a proper burial," the second soldier said, obviously trying to smoother a laugh.

"Proper burial?" was all Rab could say as he tried to size up the situation.

"Sure, you know we take all the unwanteds over to the Valley of Hinnom, say a few choice words over them and dump them for the buzzards."

"That's all for free, of course, courtesy of the Governor," the first soldier added. "If you throw in a coin or two we will give them the deluxe treatment."

Rab just looked at the two men, not sure if he should dare speak.

"With the deluxe treatment we take them over to the portion of the dump where the fires are going and put them on the burning garbage. The smoke keeps the buzzards away."

"And the fire keeps the rats away," the second soldier added.

"That way the corpses can rot in peace."

Rab's mind turned toward the Valley of Hinnom, or Gehenna as it was called. It was Jerusalem's garbage dump. Fires burned continually, fed by all kinds of useless and used up refuse disposed of by the townspeople. Fortunately the acrid smell was usually carried away from the city by the prevailing western winds, but not always. The dump was such a distasteful place its very name had come to refer to the eternal fires of hell.

Rab started to get up, but before he could the first soldier held his right hand up in a warning gesture while his left hand moved to rest on his sword handle. Rab sat back down and waited.

"Of course, there is a third option," the soldier said with a smile. "We could deputize you and leave these two …" He nodded toward the bodies of Isaac and Jonah. "in your care."

"That sounds like a good idea to me," Rab began, but before he could say any more the first soldier continued, "But there is a fee."

"For the deputizing," the second added.

Rab was so weary he did not have the energy to match wits with these Roman thugs, but neither did he have any money. Looking at the two men, he guessed they were as tired of this business as he was. He decided to call their bluff.

"You gentlemen know I would not do anything to stand in the way of your doing your duty. Why don't you just take these two with you. I can always visit them at the dump, or if not, I'll probably spend eternity with them in Gehenna.

It took only a glance at Rab's wooden smile for the soldiers to realize they were not going to get any money from the thief. They looked at each other, both shrugged and then turned back to Rab.

"We appreciate that you have given us no trouble during this ordeal, so we will deputize you anyway, without the fee. How does that sound?"

"That's fine. I'll take care of these two," Rab replied, then added, "I'll see they get a good burial."

"That's our main concern," the soldiers said together. "We'll leave them in your care," the first soldier added, as the two turned and walked away.

Rab relaxed a little as the two joined their companions and the whole squad left the hill.

Sitting alone beside his two dead friends, Rab watched the sun set. With the sun now behind the western plateau, the sky changed from a brilliant blood red to a dark crimson to a deep purple before giving up its hold on the worst day of Rab's life. He was not looking forward to spending the night on Skull Hill with two corpses. He was not looking forward to anything. Soon it was completely dark.

Totally spent and feeling he had aged years since the sun had come up, Rab tucked his arms around his chest and allowed his eyes to close, exchanging one darkness for another.

There could not be a better picture of the way I feel.

Chapter Twenty-five

The first memory Rab had of that High Sabbath was wondering what was causing the black shadows crossing between him and the noon time sun. After opening, then shading his bleary eyes, he was finally able to determine they were buzzards, lots of buzzards. Despite being bone tired, the product of rocky ground and bad dreams, he forced himself to get up. After stretching his arms and legs into action, he dragged both corpses into a nearby ditch and started covering them with rocks. Burying his friends took a lot longer than he had anticipated. That he had no words to say over Jonah except something about his failure to be a better father figure saddened him. The sorrow deepened with the realization that he did not know how to locate Jonah's real father or mother and so did not know how to inform them of their son's death.

When he looked down at Isaac's pile of rocks he said that for Isaac's sake he hoped Jesus was the real Messiah or at least that what He said about them being together in Paradise was true. Rab had to admit that against all odds, the timing of their deaths had turned out to be accurate. Afterward he did not feel up to interaction with the living, and so he found a patch of grass and collapsed again.

Frightening thoughts jarred him out of a restless sleep. He found that he was lying on his back, looking aimlessly up at the night sky. When his mind cleared he realized the stars were as bright and beautiful as he had ever seen them. Like almost every other subject, Rab had never studied the stars, learned any of their names or groups, but he had spent many nights in the open air and he liked looking up at them. It always made him feel like he was part of something bigger, maybe an insignificant part, but still a part. He also liked the orderliness they presented. They were dependable and it made him want to be that way too, although he had noticed that a few seemed to wander around more than the others.

That's like me, the wanderers, he had told himself.

One more thought entered his mind before he dozed off again. *So much for the High Sabbath!*

It wasn't his dreams that awakened Rab next. It was the violent rolling of the ground beneath him. After much effort he managed to roll over on his stomach and grasp clumps of grass. That at least gave him the illusion of control as his body was jerked furiously up and down and from side to side.

That's the second earthquake in .... Rab had no idea what time or even what day it was. After the earth stopped reeling, he rolled over on his back and lay still for a long time looking up at the dimly lit sky.

His heart rate finally slowed to normal and his mind began to function again.

It has to be sometime in the early morning of the first day of the week, Rab finally concluded. Willing himself back to reality he wondered, *What will life bring today?* Recalling the earthquake and looking in the direction of the two mounds of rocks nearby, he added with a genuine feeling of gratitude, *At least I am alive.*

He dared not move until the first rays of sunlight appeared, then standing up, he stretched and looked around. From his position he had a pretty good view of the Benjamin Road and the smaller road that ran to the north between Skull Hill and a walled garden. He was wondering where, or from whom, he might get something to eat when he noticed three women hurrying north along the smaller road, barely visible in the shadow of Skull Hill. Another glance at the few remaining stars in the sky told him that the city gates were still closed.

Being outside the city walls before dawn is dangerous, even for a man, Rab thought. *Don't you ladies know there are robbers about?*

He continued to watch them as he started moving in a direction that would allow him to intercept them. Certain they had not seen him since he too was in the shadows.

As they drew near, Rab noticed they were each carrying something that looked like jars and small sacks. He could not tell what the objects were, but as they hurried past, Rab caught the hint of a sweet scent. They did not notice him, though he was now following close enough for him to hear their conversation.

"Who will roll away the stone for us from the entrance of the tomb?" one of the women asked. The other two women shrugged their shoulders. All kept their hurried pace.

Normally Rab prided himself in being able to size up a possible heist, but today he was having difficulty focusing. First, he was not sure he wanted to rob the women, but in addition to that distraction, he thought he recognized the women as having been at the crucifixion, especially the one. They had just asked about a tomb, and then there was that smell.

That has to be perfume, Rab concluded. *That has to be worth some money.*

Rab figured it would be easy to run by the women and grab as many of the objects as possible without even slowing down. His only problem was the possibility of being identified. If he got close enough to recognize that woman, maybe she would also recognize him. Plus, it was getting lighter by the minute he realized, glancing back over his right shoulder toward Skull Hill.

He had decided to forget all but the perfume and was about to make his move when the women suddenly turned to their left and stopped at one of the gates in the wall of the garden. One of the other women pulled on the latch and pushed open the gate. The other two women stepped aside. Rab did recognize the woman and despite himself he breathed her name.

Magdelena? Mary Magdelene! Now he remembered. She was one of the wealthy women he had robbed a few years back during a time when he was robbing rich but weak people. He had always targeted the rich, but it had become too risky going after businessmen, so for a period of time he picked out easier prey, mostly women. He'd noticed Magdelena (as he called her) while studying Joanna, the wife of the manager of King Herod's household. Joanna had all but made herself a target because of her easy access to and eagerness to spend Herod's money. Joanna and Magdelena were shopping partners.

In his study of Magdelena he learned she had come to Jerusalem from Magdela, a small fishing village on the eastern shore of the Sea of Galilee. When Rab also learned she was the widow of a successful fisherman, and now lived alone, he had decided to rob her. She fit the weak profile better than Joanna. In fact, he had observed her over a number of days and nights and noticed that she was prone to throw tantrums of some sort. These rants would be followed by periods of extreme quiet, even reclusiveness. At other times she would storm around her house having animated conversations, into thin air it appeared to Rab.

The robbery had been straight forward and had gone smoothly. He had waited until she had gone shopping and had broken into her home. He was disappointed in the scarcity of jewelry he found, barely worth his extensive scouting efforts, but took what was there. Unfortunately Magdelena had returned home earlier than expected and he passed her on the street. He was sure she got a pretty good look at him, and so he had often wondered if she realized he was the one who had robbed her.

Waiting for the other two women to go through the gate, Magdelena stepped back. As she did she glanced back in the direction the three had come. Her face was now in better light and yes, it was Mary Magdelene. For an instant their eyes met. Rab thought he saw a moment of recognition on her face, or *maybe she was just startled.* She quickly hastened the other two and herself through the gate.

Rab waited for quite a while before approaching the garden gate. He was trying to decide if he should go in or not.

It was not exactly a public place, but being a working garden meant there was business conducted there on occasion, if not this early. Then there was still the matter of food. The garden might house some dried fruit, certainly no ripe fruit this time of year. No doubt the garden's cisterns would be full to the brim. Regardless of whether he found food, the thought of a drink of water was motivation enough.

He drew the gate string and was surprised the latch released. The women had not locked the door behind them, and so he pushed it open just enough to squeeze through. He moved quickly though quietly along, staying close to the foliage on the side of the cobblestone path. He did not know where the cisterns were located, but as he looked around, he also kept his eyes open for the women.

Before rounding a curve he heard the women's voices. Rab left the path to his right and worked his way through the rows of grape vines toward the voices. He hoped the vines, filled with leaves, would allow him to get fairly close without being noticed.

"Did you see them?" Rab heard one of the women ask.

"Did you hear what they said?" another one asked.

"I did but I don't understand," the first spoke again.

It sounded like all three women were now talking at once. Rab could not understand anything, but it was obvious they were upset or excited or both.

Rab quietly moved into a position from which he could see the women. As he watched, Magdelena laid the things she was carrying on the ground beside an opening in the rock wall they were standing near. She then turned back to the women, raised her hands for quiet and said, "Let's leave the spices here and go. We can get them later."

At her suggestion, the other two placed their articles on the ground. Then all three started back up the path. Rab held his breath as the three hurried by, passing only a couple of arm's lengths from him. Before they left through the gate he heard Magdelena say, "It'll be alright."

Rab considered all he had heard, but none of it made any sense. He studied the scene for clues. What he saw was a rock wall. It had two openings in it. One was near the ground and large enough for a man to pass through, if he stooped. The smaller opening was higher up the face of the wall.

They said something about a tomb, Rab recalled. The small opening was the clincher. *Tombs usually contain a small window to allow the soul of the dead to exit, after three days, on its way to its reward,* Rab knew.

If there really is a reward? If there really is a soul? Rab had always questioned those ideas.

There was a large round stone beside the larger opening, probably the entrance. The women had stacked their articles beside it.

Maybe this will turn out alright after all, Rab thought remembering the spices. The tomb was intriguing, but the spices were the main thing. He considered whether he should take time to examine the tomb or just grab the spices and run. Years of self-preservation caused him to survey the area again before leaving his hiding place. He was glad he did, for now he was surprised to discover a Roman soldier lying on the ground almost concealed by the large stone.
Maybe it was too dark before, he told himself, hoping he wasn't losing his edge.

Looking more closely now, he spotted another soldier, and another and still another. They all appeared to be sleeping.

What are Roman soldiers doing here at this tomb? Are they guarding it? Why? If so, why are they asleep? Don't you guys know you can be executed for sleeping on the job?

Pondering the questions only confused him. He suddenly felt very irritable, and hungry and thirsty. After looking over the scene he reluctantly turned and started back the way he had come. When he came to a fork in the path he decided to follow the other fork hoping it would lead to one of the cisterns. It did and nearby he found an empty clay pot. He dipped it into the cistern and took several long drinks. He dipped the pot again and this time poured the cool water over his head and face. Finally he poured some water on the back of his neck. While wiping his face with his sleeve he noticed a small set of stairs leading up to a terrace. Noticing that the area was fairly well concealed by trees, he filled the pot again and climbed the stairs.

At the top of the terrace was a small arbor and under it a stone bench built into the wall of the garden. Rab slumped onto the bench, took another long drink and looked over the garden. Even though he was above ground level, he felt he was far enough away from the path to be safe from the soldiers should they awaken and exit the garden. He relaxed and continued to look around. From his vantage point Rab could tell that the garden was well maintained and beautiful. In addition to the grape vines there were several old olive trees. The most spectacular however were the almond trees. Their full canopies of white and pink washed Rab with a sense of beauty and peace. His serenity was short-lived, however because his gaze had taken in the entire garden from left to right and now he was looking over the wall.

Directly across the street was Skull Hill. The contrast was startling. From this viewpoint the cave holes in the side of the rock looked so obviously like a human skull that Rab inadvertently drew in a deep breath. All of the events of the last two days replayed in his mind: his well planned robbery in the market gone bad, his arrest, his imprisonment in Caiaphas' dungeon, his slaying of the young Jewish guard, his trial before Pilate, his release.

Rab suddenly realized all of his thoughts were about himself. Sitting there staring at Skull Hill he could clearly see the three crosses still standing in place.

Isaac and Jonah died on those stakes, and they are buried just over that hill, he slumped a little lower on the bench. His attention now turned to the middle cross. Rab studied it because somehow it looked different than the other two.

The sign! The sign is still there, Rab realized.

"Jesus the Nazarene. The King of the Jews!" Rab said right out loud. "Man, you sure knew how to anger them, even while dying. Who were you, really?"

Rab recalled his face to face meeting in the prison. He blushed at the memory of Jesus' obvious knowledge of him and even more his deep concern for him.

He showed more concern for everyone than He did for Himself, Rab had to acknowledge. *Even on the cross he encouraged Isaac and he took care of his mother.*

Now the questions began to race through his mind: *Why did that Centurion say 'He was the Son of God?' What did Mary Magdelene have to do with Him? And who was that rich man that offered to bury Him? Where did they take His body?*

"That's it," he realized out loud as his eyes fell on the rock wall on the far side of the garden. He could see only the top portion of the wall extending above the trees, but he recalled the whole wall. "That is Jesus' tomb."

Thinking back over the events of the morning Rab wondered, *"What is going on?"*

He had to know the answer. And so, after taking one more look at Skull Hill, he pulled himself off the bench, descended the steps and hurried toward the tomb. He decided that he could do so in plain sight since the only crime he might be committing was trespassing.

The Romans won't care about that, he assured himself. Even so when he heard the gate slam open against the garden wall and the sound of men running, he immediately jumped into the vineyard. As he made his way quietly back to his observation spot, he could hear the men racing down the path.

One of the men arrived first. Either not seeing or ignoring the soldiers he stopped directly in front of the tomb entrance and peered in. A second, older man, came up behind and without hesitation disappeared into the tomb. After a few moments the younger man followed. It seemed like a long time before they came out. When they did Rab recognized the younger man as the man at the cross whom Jesus had placed in charge of caring for his mother. He did not recognize the older man, nor could he understand anything the two said. However, their expressions, like those of the women before them, communicated confusion as they made their way back toward the garden gate. Something had happened, but Rab could not tell what it was.

Rab decided it was time to leave too. He looked once more at the tomb, then the spices and finally the soldiers. The soldiers were still sleeping soundly so he decided to take the spices. But before he could move, he was surprised by a lone woman who quietly approached the tomb. He watched as she stopped before the opening. He thought he could hear her weeping. Finally she stooped and looked inside the tomb. He heard a man's voice coming from inside the tomb, but could not understand anything that was said. Wanting to hear, Rab chanced getting closer and began picking his way through the vines. He stopped as the woman emerged backward from the tomb, still looking in. To his surprise, Rab now noticed a man standing on the path behind the woman, his back to him.

Where did he come from?

The man said to her, "Woman, why are you weeping? Whom are you seeking?"

"Sir," she pleaded, turning around quickly, "if you have carried Him away, tell me where you have laid Him, and I will take Him away."

It's Magdelena! Rab gasped, almost aloud.

"Mary!" the man said to her.

Startled, she looked more closely at Him. Rab watched her face. First he saw puzzlement, then recognition, followed immediately by astonishment. Suddenly she ran to the man, threw herself at His feet and encircled His ankles with her arms. She exclaimed, "Teacher, Teacher."

Rab watched as the man reached over and gently, but firmly pulled her up by the shoulders. Rab expected the man to embrace her, but instead he held her at arm's length, steadied her and said, "Stop clinging to Me, for I have not yet ascended to the Father; but go to My brothers and say to them, 'I ascend to my Father and your Father, and My God and your God'."

Wiping tears from her eyes with her shawl, Magdelena took a few steps back from the man, hesitated and then started past him up the path. Rab now could see her face. On it was the brightest, most beautiful smile he had ever seen. A wave of emotion completely unfamiliar to him forged through his body as he watched her run past. He could not take his eyes off her. Even after she was out of sight he listened to the diminishing sound of her footsteps. He heard the garden gate shut. When he reluctantly turned back, the man she had been talking with was gone.

After a while he glanced at the spices, shook his head, turned and quietly made his way through the vines to the path and then walked quickly to the gate. Once on the street he breathed a sigh of relief and turned south toward the city.

It was still early and so the road was fairly deserted. Rab was relieved. He did not know where he was going to go. He thought about his house, but there wasn't any food there. Besides it was all the way across town, plus Isaac and Jonah's things were there. He just wasn't ready to face that.

Chapter Twenty-six

"I think I am going crazy," Rab said as he picked up a rock, threw it and watched it disappear over the side of the hill. Absently, he picked up another one and threw it even harder. "I tell you guys I really thought about going straight, even tried it for a few days. I even went over to the Temple and offered a sacrifice. I know what both of you are thinking, but it's true. Those phony priests took my offering, but when I told them I was going to go straight … get a regular job, they laughed me out of the courtyard. If there is a god I hope he is not like them."

Rab was sitting on Skull Hill several paces from the graves of his two friends. "I did find a job moving stones for a builder. That's why I haven't been here for the last two days. I am too old for that, but I don't know what else to do. Jonah, just like I told you, 'Once a thief always a thief!' I'll probably join you guys here someday."

He sat there a few more minutes as a warm breeze blew over him. He glanced at the sun and stood up. He wiped his forehead with his sleeve then allowed his arm to remain over his nose and mouth. As he turned to go back down the hill he mumbled into his sleeve, "You guys are beginning to stink."

As he walked down the hill he glanced over to the wall that enclosed the garden tomb. Rab had not figured it out, but there was something about that place that drew him. It may have simply been the bit of serenity he had felt while drinking the cool water on the terrace overlooking the beauty of the garden. It could have been the hope he saw in the attractive smile of Magdelena as she ran past him that day. Maybe it was the unsolved mysteries of the tomb and that man. Maybe it was the possibility of finding the store of spices. He did not know, but found himself walking across the street and toward the garden gate.

Rab felt a rush, similar, if less intense; to the way he

always did before a robbery, as he pulled the gate latch and let himself into the garden. He stepped into the coolness and felt almost at home as he walked quietly down the path. The garden seemed to be empty so when he came to the fork, he turned and made his way to the cistern. As before he filled a pot, climbed the stairs and sat down on the terrace bench. He took several long drinks as he looked across the street at Skull Hill. Again he noted that the sign which had been above Jesus' head was still there. Absently he used his big toes to work his sandals, first one then the other, off his feet. He was just about to turn back and pour cool water on his feet when he heard, "I'll do that for you."

Rab jumped up, turned toward the voice and took as defensive a posture as best he could, standing bare foot and with a pot as his only weapon. He had to look down to find the man standing on one of the lower steps.

Rab quickly assessed that he had little hope of running, being barefoot and with the man blocking the way. But, if it came to a fight, his position on the terrace above the man gave him the advantage. When Rab realized the man was much older, late fifties, maybe early sixties, he relaxed a little. When he spoke to the man his voice was calm.

"Who are you? What do you want?"

"I apologize," the man said. "I did not mean to startle you."

The smile on his face seems genuine, Rab thought, his heartbeat almost back to normal.

"To answer your questions, my name is Joseph and what I want is to welcome you to my garden," the man said softly and deliberately. "As an expression of my hospitality I would be honored to wash your feet."

The man's face, with its pleasant smile and clear eyes, did not seem to be harboring any deceit, at least none that was obvious to Rab as he studied it. Nonetheless he kept the pot poised in front of his chest. The man's request to wash his feet had seemed genuine, but was difficult to process. Rab knew the simplest form of hospitality was to have a servant wash the feet of one's guests. With sandals, one's feet become hot and dusty. This simple act of kindness was especially refreshing. Still, in this setting, it did not make much sense.

"You want to wash my feet?" Rab finally asked slowly. "Why would you do that?"

"Again I apologize," the man said, still smiling. "If you would feel more comfortable I would be happy to call one of the servants to do it. I offered to do so simply because my Master said we should look for ways to serve others. Then in one of His last acts of kindness, He washed the feet of His followers. I was not present at the time, but greatly desire to become like Him in every way I can," he explained.

Lowering the water pot to his side Rab said stiffly, "I am fine, I do not need you ... or your servants ... to wash my feet."

The man nodded his head in agreement as he watched Rab sit down on the bench and begin putting on his sandals. "That is perfectly understandable," the man said, "but please do not feel that you have to leave. You are more than welcome to stay and enjoy the beauty of my garden."

Looking over his sandals as he strapped them, and without being too obvious, Rab studied the man before him. He noticed the man's robe looked familiar. When he was finished with his shoes he stood up, looked down at the man and asked, "Joseph! Did you say your name is Joseph?"

Joseph nodded.

"Have we met?" As soon as the words were out of his mouth Rab realized who the man was.

"You were at the crucifixion. You are the man who took down Jesus' body."

"You are correct," Joseph said, nodding. "And you were also at the crucifixion."

Rab suddenly became uncomfortable. He did not want to reveal his identity. He turned to pick up the water pot.

"It is okay. I know who you are as well, Jesus Bar-Abbas," Joseph said calmly.

Rab turned back to him, but before he could respond, Joseph continued, "I saw you at the crucifixion. I also saw you at the trial before Pilate when you were set free. A great gift, freedom," Joseph concluded more to himself than to Rab.

"If you know who I am why did you welcome me in here and why did you offer to wash my feet?" Rab blurted out.

"I told you," Joseph answered. "I am following the example of my Master, Jesus."

Rab was not sure what to say. Finally he thought of something, "I met Jesus before the trial."

"On one of his ministry trips?" Joseph asked surprised.

Rab looked put off by the interruption.

"I apologize," Joseph said bowing slightly. "Please continue."

"I was in Caiaphas' dungeon when the priests brought Jesus in. It sounded like a trial, if you could call it that … more like a beating. Jesus was so badly bruised it was difficult to look at his face. The priests and lawyers on the Council sure did themselves proud with Him."

Rab was surprised he was saying so much to this stranger. Even more of a surprise was Joseph's response. He had looked down and then away. Finally he said, "I am a member of the Council."

Rab's face must have registered alarm, because Joseph raised his hands in a placating gesture and said, "No, no, it's quite alright. You are correct; that trial was completely wrong. In fact it was actually illegal, since it was at night," he admitted. "There were a few of us who had come to believe that Jesus was the long awaited Messiah. Sadly, in order to keep peace with the High Priest, we just went along with the process, saying very little and doing even less."

Again he hung his head. "An innocent man died."

Emboldened by the man's contrition, Rab blurted out, "How do you know He was innocent? He is not innocent if he is supposed to be the Messiah, and yet dies like that with the Romans still in charge, and in league with those crooked priests. He's no more innocent than the other would be messiahs who have come and gone." As the words poured out, feelings buried by the events of the last few days now came back to life. "And He's not innocent if a lot of innocent people die just because He is born," Rab concluded angrily.

He prepared himself for Joseph to become defensive. Instead Joseph studied Rab and then quietly asked, "What innocent people?"

Rab looked back into Joseph's face. What he saw was an older man looking back at him, expressing what appeared to be a genuine interest. Then, once more, Rab noticed Joseph's robe. It was not gaudy, but it was definitely not cheap either. Before answering, Rab allowed his gaze to wander over the beautiful garden from his left to his right. He took a deep breath and smelled the flowering trees.

How can this guy, who lives so well with his fancy garden and nice clothes, have any idea about, much less interest in me, he wondered. His gaze made it around to the wall and then beyond ... to Skull Hill. *That's where my friends are,* Rab reminded himself. *That's where I belong too. What's the point?* he sighed.

But as he looked once more at Joseph, he saw that the older man had not gotten bored, or tired. He still seemed to want to know. *Oh well, for what it's worth.*

"The innocent people I am talking about are my father and mother. I never knew them," Rab began. "They died trying to hide me from Herod's soldiers when Jesus was born."

He continued telling the story as he knew it. Somewhere in the middle of the telling, Joseph came up the stairs and sat down across from Rab on the bench. That act of interest encouraged Rab to continue to talk about his life. He was careful to not incriminate himself with too many details, but he talked more to Joseph than he had to any other person in his life. It was strange because, as he began he was extremely angry, blaming God and Jesus, for every bad thing that had happened. He had included the story of his name, and wanting to live up to that. He also told of his encounter with Jesus in the dungeon, and his surprise at being released at the trial, and his sorrow at the cruel way his friends had been killed. As he continued, his anger turned to confusion, wondering about Jesus' promise to take Isaac to Paradise. Then, looking past Joseph to Skull Hill he felt sad. Rab was careful to hold back enough to keep from shaming himself openly, but that familiar, loathsome feeling lurked just below the surface.

Throughout the whole story, Joseph never took his eyes off Rab. When Rab finished Joseph said to him, "I cannot imagine how painful it must have been for you to have never known your father and mother. Nor can I even picture how difficult it was for you to have had to provide for yourself from such an early age."

Rab did not respond. He just continued to look at Skull Hill. After a pause Joseph spoke again, softly, "But I do know something about losing loved ones, innocent ones, young ones."

Rab looked at him.

"You see ..." Joseph began then stopped. "How should I address you?"

"Huh?" Rab asked.

"Your name is Jesus, but what should I call you?" Joseph asked.

"Most call me Rab."

"Rab. Okay!" Joseph said, then added. "Is that what you want to be called?"

After hesitating for a long time, Rab finally said, "I prefer to be called Joshua."

"Okay, Joshua," Joseph began. "I was going to tell you that I know the pain of losing those close to you, particularly young ones. You mentioned the loss of your parents during Herod's murdering of the innocent children around Bethlehem." He then paused for a moment to compose himself. "Herod murdered eight of our grandchildren, and not just the boys. Sometimes his soldiers did not take time to check; when they came into a village they just killed all the young children."

Rab could see the pain in the old man's eyes.

"The prophet Jeremiah," Joseph started to say, but stopped when he saw Rab roll his eyes.

Rab was embarrassed at his own rudeness and quickly apologize, "I'm sorry. It's just that I don't have much use for prophets and preachers."

Instead of getting defensive, Joseph smiled and replied, "I know what you mean. The first prophet of Israel comes from our area and everybody keeps looking for the next great prophet. Needless to say over my life I have heard more than my share of preaching. Some of it was really boring, but some of it was pretty interesting stuff."

"Again, I am sorry," Rab said. "What were you going to say about Jeremiah?"

"I was just going to say that several hundred years before Herod killed the children the prophet Jeremiah said it would happen."

"Really?" Rab asked.

"Yes," and then Joseph quoted the prophet.
 'Thus says the LORD,
  'A voice is heard in Ramah ... ,'
That's where I am from, Joseph interjected, and Rab nodded in comprehension. Joseph continued,
 ' ... Lamentation and bitter weeping.
 Rachel is weeping for her children;
 She refuses to be comforted for her children.
  Because they are no more.'"

Rab was still considering the words and did not say anything.

"As you may know, Joshua," Joseph continued after a moment, "Rachel was the mother of Benjamin whose land includes Jerusalem. About the time you were born, King Herod heard that a new king of the Jews had been born. Because of his fear of the new king, Herod killed children not only in Bethlehem but also in parts of Benjamin. Rachel represents all the mothers (and fathers) whose children were murdered."

Rab had never thought much about others who had lost children in those days of slaughter. It was obvious that Joseph, and no doubt his wife and their own children, had suffered greatly at Herod's wicked lunacy. He appreciated the kindness that Joseph had shown to him, but something about the story did not make sense to him.

"I'm sorry, Joseph, but I don't get it," Rab began tentatively. "You said, 'Thus says the LORD.' If the LORD knew hundreds of years ahead of time that Herod was going to do this, why didn't God just stop him? Why doesn't he stop all the killing?" Gaining courage from Joseph's silence he continued, "If He is really God Almighty, why doesn't' He just stop all the pain?"

Joseph did not respond immediately and Rab allowed his gaze to wander again past Joseph's somber face to Skull Hill. He focused once more on the three crosses. He thought of Jonah's fury and his cursing until the end. He remembered Isaac's prayers, even on his cross. Again he looked at the sign that had been above Jesus' head, "Jesus the Nazarene. The King of the Jews!"

Suddenly feeling very weary of having so many more questions than he had answers, he looked back at Joseph and asked, "You and the others took Jesus' body from the cross. What did you do with it?"

"Come, I'll show you," Joseph replied. He stood up and started down the steps. Rab also got up and walked down the steps. Neither man said anything as Rab followed Joseph down the path. As they rounded the bend in the path, Rab began to scour the area.

The spices are gone, he noted ruefully. *But so are the soldiers.*

As they approached the rock wall Joseph pointed to it and explained, "I had this tomb constructed recently. When Jesus was crucified I felt I should lay Him in it. Inside here," he said pointing to the entrance, "is where we laid Him."

Rab paused

"It's okay," Joseph said. "Look for yourself,"

Rab hesitantly stepped to the entrance, bent over and looked inside. The cool air was refreshing on his face. The smell was surprisingly pleasant and so he took a step inside. Once his eyes adjusted, there was enough light from the small opening above for him to see. He quickly realized the entire structure had been hollowed out of the solid rock cliff. There was a smaller entrance room and then a larger room to the right. In that room were three shelves hollowed into the rock. Two were empty but one had a folded cloth lying along its entire length. There was also another band of cloth, rolled up and lying at one end. Along the length of the cloth Rab could just make out what looked like piles of sand. *Perfume! Lot's of it. That's the reason for the pleasant aroma.* After scanning both areas again, Rab backed out and turned around. Shielding his eyes from the sun he looked at Joseph and asked, "Where is He?"

Chapter Twenty-seven

"Where is He?" Joseph repeated. "That is a good question."

Rab was not sure how to respond. Finally he said, "You just said you buried Jesus in your tomb, there," pointing to the doorway of the tomb. "Right?"

"Not exactly; I didn't say I buried him. My purpose was to lay Him in the tomb, not bury Him." Joseph said.

"I don't understand," Rab responded. "What's the difference?"

When Joseph did not answer, Rab asked, "Was Jesus dead or not?"

"Absolutely He was dead," declared Joseph. "You saw the soldiers pierce his side and the water and blood flow out. That spear went right through his heart. He was dead alright."

"Then you buried Him," Rab said conclusively.

"Not exactly," Joseph said again. "What I did was lay Him in my tomb, not bury Him."

"What's the difference?" Rab asked again, this time showing more confusion than frustration.

"The difference is that I expected Jesus to come back to life," Joseph explained.

"You expected Him to come back to life," Rab asked incredulously, "That's about the craziest thing I have ever heard. Why would you expect Him to come back to life?"

"It does sound crazy doesn't it?" Joseph conceded, "But let me explain. I have spent my life reading and studying the ancient writings." Seeing the puzzled look on Joshua's face, he explained, "The Scriptures: the Law, the Prophets, Psalms, Proverbs."

Rab rolled his eyes, but Joseph continued. "I love them dearly, and unlike some of my colleagues, I believe they are inspired by God and completely accurate, both in their recording of history and in the prophecies telling God's plans for the future."

At this Rab again made a look of disbelief.

"But, and here's the key," Joseph continued, "to really understand them you have to take them all. You can't hold to some and leave the rest. Here's my point. In my studies I learned that the Messiah of God would come and bring peace, but not in the way most believe. Most think the Messiah will come in military power and set His people free by force."

"That's what I believe," Rab interjected.

"Most do, and that picture is found in Scripture," Joseph agreed. "He is described as a conquering hero who will bring peace to the world ... but not at first. This is the part most people miss. He is also described as a servant, a suffering servant who will come and demonstrate the love of God with his life and then he will suffer and die."

"What good would that do?" Rab asked.

"A lot, but first I need to add that after he dies he will rise from the dead."

"So then can come back a second time?" Rab asked skeptically.

"That is exactly what the Scriptures teach," Joseph replied. "The first time he comes will be to serve and to die. The second time he comes will be to rule."

What Joseph was telling him sounded vaguely familiar to Rab. *Where have I heard that before? In the dungeon?* He felt his emotions rising as he tried to recall Jesus' words about His Father sending Him to earth to die. What kind of father does that? He had wanted to know. This was not the kind of father he had ever imagined.

"If you are telling me that God sent Jesus down here to earth to die, what kind of cruel God is that?" Rab demanded, turning on his heels and starting up the path.

"Wait, Joshua. Don't go. Please let me finish," Joseph pleaded. "It was for love."

"That doesn't sound like love to me," Rab shouted over his shoulder.

"It was for you, Joshua," Joseph shouted back, "You, of all people should understand this."

Rab stopped in his tracks, and whipped around. "Me? Why me? Why me of all people?"
He was working hard to hold his anger in check. "And why should I know anything about how a father's love works. I didn't have a father, remember? If your story is true then thanks to his father, my father got killed," Rab looked around and lowered his voice and said, "I know a lot about killing, but I don't know much about it being as an act of love, especially if it is your own son you are killing. What kind of father does that?"

Rab was breathing hard. One part of him wanted to run out of the garden and get as far away from this crazy talk as possible. Another part of him really hoped that whatever Joseph was peddling was real. For a while he could not decide what to do. Finally he looked back at the old man.

"A father who loves his own son so much that he would like to have many, many more sons just like him," Joseph replied quietly.

"What are you talking about?"

Joseph walked across the clearing and sat down on a bench beside the path. Rab wanted to turn around and run out, but despite himself, he liked the old man and was grateful to him for his kindness. He might read the Scriptures, but he was different. He didn't seem to be a hypocrite like the priests, and he didn't seem crazy like Isaac. He couldn't decide what to do. Finally, he shrugged his shoulders, walked over to where Joseph was sitting and sat down on a bench on the other side of the path.

"Okay, let me see if I get this," Rab began. "You say that God has a son and he loves his son so he wants to have more sons." He looked over at Joseph who was nodding. "So to have more sons he made us ... men?"

"That's correct," Joseph said.

"I'm not anything like what I think God's son should

be," Rab said surprised at his own honesty. "I don't know anyone who is, maybe you, but certainly not my friends, and not your friends, those priests out there. They're the worst of the bunch."

"Joshua, all of us want to compare ourselves with others. If we want to feel good about ourselves, we can find someone we are better than. If we want to feel bad, we simply find someone we are worse than," Joseph began. "If we want to know what God thinks about us, we compare ourselves to God's purpose for our lives, becoming like his own Son. And on that count, we all fall very far short. No man has ever qualified on his own to become one of God's sons."

"That's because it is impossible," Rab said suddenly,

"No, it's not impossible," Joshua corrected, "but it is very difficult and you would have to rely on God's help every step of the way."

"Nobody does that," Rab exclaimed.

"You are exactly right, and so we all miss the mark and we all need to be forgiven," Joseph said quietly.

Joseph's words caused Rab to think back. "Is that what Jesus meant when he prayed, 'Father, forgive them?' We keep messing it up. So God had to send His son to earth to die so the rest of us sons …

"Potential sons," Joseph corrected.

"Okay, potential sons could be forgiven. Is that it?" Joseph nodded.

"So let's say you are right about all this," Rab began again. "All this forgiveness depends on him actually being the Son of God, not just some nice guy who happened to make those crooked priests mad at Him."

Joseph smiled, "You are right again. If Jesus was just another man he could pay for his own sins, but if He is the Son of God, he could pay for all our sins."

"So how do you know that He is really the Son of God?" Rab asked.

Joseph's smile turned into a sly grin. "Well I figured

that if he is truly the Son of God then what he said about dying would happen, but so would the part about Him rising from the dead on the third day."

"So you thought all along Jesus was going to rise from the dead," Rab asked.

"Well, not all along, but for a while now. First of all, if you read the ancient writings, sorry, Scriptures carefully you will see the Messiah's death and resurrection. Anyone can say they are the Messiah, but if someone lived like the Messiah, died like the Messiah and then was raised from the dead, that would be pretty good proof that He is the Messiah, don't you think?" Joseph asked.

Rab found himself nodding in agreement.

"Okay look at his life. For starters, Jesus taught with great authority," Joseph said holding up his thumb as he began to count his points. "Unlike the rest of the teachers who simply quote others, Jesus would say, 'It is written, but I say...' None of the Council lawyers could catch Him in a single misstatement."

Rab recalled how Jesus seemed to know an awfully lot about him, though they had never met before.

Extending his index finger Joseph said, "Next, he healed thousands of people."

"He healed my friend, Isaac," Rab inserted. "Then He told him to sin no more."

"Okay," Joseph agreed and then extending his middle finger he continued, "In addition He has demonstrated his power over evil spirits by driving them out of people and removing their torment."

"I know some people who probably have demons, but don't know anyone who had any thrown out of them," Rab said thoughtfully.

"Did you see the women at the cross?" Joseph asked.

"Was one of them Jesus' mother," Rab asked.

"Yes, that's right, but another was Mary Magdelene."

Rab's heart skipped a beat at the mention of the name.

For a moment he was afraid that Joseph might suggest he meet her. *What if she can identify me as the one who robbed her house?*

"She can tell you her story of how Jesus cast seven demons out of her."

Rab did not think he was entirely successful in showing no reaction, but if Joseph noticed the slight change in Joshua's expression, he did not respond. Instead he extended another finger and continued, "Jesus also raised several people from the dead."

Rab did not respond so Joseph continued, "It became obvious to me that Jesus had power from God to do these things." Extending the little finger he concluded, "Add to that, for many months now He has been saying He will suffer, die and rise from the dead."

"So then you did believe He would rise from the dead?" Rab asked again.

"I did. Months ago I realized what was going to happen."

"So you bought this garden and had this tomb built to be used for Jesus," Rab interrupted.

"Yes," Joseph nodded.

But something wasn't quite adding up. When he realized what it was Rab asked, "So if you believed Jesus was going to rise from the dead, why did you put all those spices around his body?"

"You are a bright young man," Joseph began. "I did not plan to. When I took Jesus down from the cross I used only a linen cloth, something like a bed sheet, to wrap His body and a cloth for His head. However, I have a friend, Nicodemus, who is also a member of the Council who opposed Jesus' death. After everyone else had gone, he came to the tomb to help me with the stone, but he brought a lot of spices. We argued over whether to use them or not, but I decided it did not matter and gave in to him. We put the spices around and then rolled the stone over the entrance."

Joseph got up, walked toward and pointed to the large stone. Rab followed behind. Joseph looked back and when he saw the frown on Rab's face he explained further, "You can see that the stone is designed to roll in this channel to cover the entrance."

Rab looked at the large stone and the stone channel it sat in and nodded.

"We had to do it all rather hurriedly because the sun was setting and we had to be finished before dark, the beginning of the High Sabbath."

"So what happened to the body?" Rab asked again.

"I'm coming to that, but first you need to understand something else."

Rab waited.

"When some of the Council members reported to the High Priest that Jesus was dead, Caiaphas remembered that Jesus had said, 'After three days I will rise again'. Caiaphas believed Jesus was a deceiver so he took a delegation to Governor Pilate. He told the Governor that some of Jesus' followers might come to the tomb, steal His body, and then say that Jesus had risen from the dead. He warned Pilate that if that happened the last deception would be greater than the first. Pilate ordered a squad of soldiers to the tomb, to seal it and guard it until after the third day."

That explains the soldiers, Rab thought, *but not why they were asleep.* "What happened then," he asked.

"That's when everything gets a little confusing," Joseph said. "We know the soldiers came and sealed the tomb. In fact, if you look above the entrance up there," he said pointing, "you can see what is left of the Roman's wax seal." He then pointed to the stone and said, "And you can see the other part of the seal here too."

Rab walked over to the stone and examined it.

"But look at this," Joseph said pointing up at the rock wall again. "The soldiers must have really wanted this tomb to stay sealed because they drove a metal spike right into the wall so that the stone could not be rolled away."

Rab looked up and could see what looked like a large nail buried in a crack in the rock and sheered off even with the front of the wall.

"That looks like a pretty sturdy piece of metal. How did it get cut off like that?" Rab asked.

"We don't know for sure," Joseph said. "No one came to the tomb on the High Sabbath, but early on the first day of the week, some of the women who had helped us bury Jesus came. They brought more spices to complete the burial."

Rab started to ask why they brought spices, but decided to wait.

"You see, they were not aware of Pilate's order to seal the tomb or of the soldiers guarding it. They were mainly concerned about how they would roll away the stone to be able to go inside."

Rab struggled whether or not he should tell Joseph he had witnessed what happened next.

"Why did they want to go inside," Rab asked.

"They too did not believe Jesus would rise from the dead. After we placed the body, they had left before Nicodemus came with the spices so they thought more spices would be needed. But when they got here they discovered the stone rolled away and ..." again Joseph paused. "They saw an angel sitting on the stone."

Rab had been examining the stone and tomb more closely, but at these words his head involuntarily jerked toward Joseph. *Well I thought I saw what happened next. How did I miss seeing an angel?* He then tried to recall how long he had waited outside the gate before coming in.

Seeing Joshua's reaction, Joseph assumed he did not believe in angels. He asked directly, "Do you believe there are angels, Joshua?"

Rab slowly nodded his head, more to keep the story moving than out of conviction. It was enough for Joseph and he continued. "They said his appearance was like lightning and his clothes were as white as snow."

"Where was the angel?" Rab asked.

Joseph could not tell whether Joshua really believed him or not, but he answered, "He was sitting on the stone. He told them not to be afraid, that Jesus had risen from the dead. He then instructed them to look inside the tomb. When they looked inside they saw the linen cloth lying on the shelf and the head wrapping lying close by. Suddenly two angels appeared in the tomb and explained in more detail what had happened. Then they instructed the women to go and tell Jesus' followers. The women left and reported what they had seen and heard to two of his followers. The men immediately came to see for themselves."

Rab had been listening carefully to see if Joseph's story lined up with what he had observed. It certainly seemed to, except for the angel part which he could have missed. Now he turned his attention back to the tomb and the stone.

"Why did you design the tomb like this, with the huge stone door?" Rab asked.

"Well, first the stone is very heavy so not just anyone will bother trying to move it. But with this design, the tomb can be opened much more easily than one where a person is buried in the ground," Joseph explained.

"So you wanted to be able to open the tomb so Jesus could get out?" Rab asked with a note of sarcasm.

"Actually, I am embarrassed to agree that was my plan," Joseph began, another smile crossing his lips, "but I found out later Jesus didn't need the stone rolled away to leave the tomb."

Rab frowned.

"Remember Joshua, we had an earthquake that morning so either the angels or the earthquake rolled the stone away, breaking both the wax seal I showed you and the iron spike the Romans had used to secure it in place," Joseph explained.

The explanation did not quite satisfy him so Rab

asked, "Did you say Jesus didn't need the stone moved to get out of the tomb?"

"That's right," Joseph replied.

"What do you mean and how do you know that?" Rab asked.

Joseph pondered the question for a minute then said, "If I told you, it would be second-hand. Why don't I introduce you to the one who explained it to me? In fact, why don't I arrange for you to meet some of Jesus' other followers. I mentioned Mary Magdalene: it would be good for you to hear her story."

As much as he was beginning to like Joseph, the idea of meeting Magdelena was still frightening, to say the least. After thinking about this for a moment, Rab realized he was not ready to commit to meet with any of Joseph's friends so he just shrugged his shoulders. He then remembered the question he wanted to ask. "I assume you are thinking that God, either by an angel or with the earthquake ..."

"Rolled the stone away," Joseph interrupted, with a broad smile on his face. "Maybe the angel caused the earthquake."

It was obvious to Rab that Joseph was really into this, but he was still skeptical. "Here's my question," he began. "You haven't explained it yet, but if you believe that Jesus did not need the doorway opened to get out, why roll the stone away?"

After a moment's reflection they both spoke at the same time, "So we could see in." They each looked at the other and then both laughed out loud.

Chapter Twenty-eight

It felt good to laugh. Rab could not remember the last time he had felt light-hearted enough to smile, much less actually laugh out loud. He knew the feeling wouldn't last, but for now, as he walked back toward the city, he felt better than he could remember. Even glimpsing Skull Hill on his way out of the garden had not dampened his mood. As he walked, he tried to analyze why he felt so good. He certainly had enjoyed getting to know Joseph, and could not help thinking, *So that's what it is like to have an older man show an interest in you.* He even allowed himself to imagine what it would have been like as a boy to have had a father like Joseph. He thought too, if he ever had any kids, he would like to learn how to be a father like Joseph. Even realizing the odds against that were pretty high, did not dampen his mood … for long.

He also thought a lot about the things the older man had said. They certainly made sense, especially if Jesus had done all of the things Joseph mentioned. The tomb was empty, and Joseph did not appear to be the kind of man that would stage a heist. The rest of Jesus' followers might, but there seemed to be two problems with that. First, they would have to be fooling Joseph. Second, making up a story like that could get them crucified too. *Who wants to die for a known lie?*

Rab conceded that he may have allowed his own anger to cloud his judgment back in the dungeon. He recalled that his anger took over when he had learned of the connection between Jesus' birth and the death of his family. Even if he was wrong then, he was still not buying the resurrection story just yet. There probably was some other explanation for the empty tomb. If so then Jesus, despite what His followers believed, would be just another false messiah. He would be a faker and certainly not the Son of God.

On the other hand, Rab had to admit, *Jesus did not fit*

the pattern of a false messiah or any deliverer I have ever heard about. They all came gathering armies to overthrow the Romans or whoever was in power. Not Jesus, He came forgiving the very soldiers who put Him on the cross to die.

He wondered, *Would the real Son of God forgive Romans, particularly soldiers?* He remembered that Jesus had said something about dying to defeat His enemies and Jonah had yelled back that "It was the enemy that needed to do the dying!" or something like that.

Jesus was different. That's for sure! Rab concluded. *But was He the Son of God? Joseph is convinced He is. I need another opinion; someone who is more neutral.*

He was walking down El Wadi Road when he suddenly stopped in his tracks. He glanced up at the walls of Jerusalem a few blocks to his left, then at the higher walls near the Temple. *The priests in the Temple certainly are not neutral,* he assured himself. *They even hired Romans soldiers to guard the tomb.* Finally his eyes came to rest on the walls of the Fortress of Antonia.

"That's it," Rab shouted. "I'll go see what that Centurion has to say about all of this."

Immediately the thought of going once more into the Fortress of Antonia caused him to pause. He assured himself, however, that he had been pardoned, was a free man and could approach the authorities with no fear. That thought gave him a boldness that was not of his own making. It was simply a condition of his freedom. He liked the feeling and picked up his pace as he turned east and headed toward the Fort.

I wonder if this is what it is like to be pardoned by God and know you can approach Him with no fear? Was this what Joseph was talking about? I hope he is right, but how can I know for sure?

It felt strange going to ask a Roman officer for advice on spiritual matters. Well he wasn't actually going to ask for advice, but simply his opinion of what happened at the crucifixion and at the tomb. Rab wasn't sure how he would be able to make contact with the man, and for the first time in a long time he breathed a silent prayer that if God wanted him to learn something from the Centurion that the officer would somehow be available. He then decided the best chance would be to go to the Praetorium and inquire. As he entered the gate, his former boldness waned. Nevertheless he ascended the stairs two at a time and walked out into the area of Jerusalem controlled entirely by the Romans. And they were everywhere.

He recalled that the last time he was there had been really intense. He had entered as a convicted criminal facing death and walked out a stunned, but free man. Rab made his way past the many shops and over to the Praetorium. Along the way he saw numerous soldiers, but decided to wait until he got to the Praetorium to inquire. Hopefully the officer he was seeking was stationed at the Fort and did not work directly for the Governor. Since the feast was over, if he was over the Governor's personal guard, he would probably already have accompanied Pilate back to his home in Caesarea.

"Hey you," Rab heard from behind. "What are you doing here?" Again, louder this time, "You, I'm speaking to you. Don't ignore me. Do you want to go back to prison?"

At this Rab stopped and turned slowly, his eyes scouring the area for a place to run. He found the source of the voice, two soldiers approaching him, their spears angled down at the ready.

One was about his own age and the other somewhat younger. Rab still had his dagger, and knew that if he used it against these two, he probably would die at worst and get put in prison at best, then die. Crucifixion would be the worst.

That would be one way to see the Centurion, Rab considered. He then made a decision based on the truth he knew rather than the emotions he felt. He relaxed, brought his hands into full view and smiled at the two soldiers as they drew nearer. He now recognized the older one as having been on the crucifixion squad, maybe the younger one too.

"I am certainly glad to see you," Rab said with a slight nod of his head. "I need your assistance, please."

Taken aback by his manner, the soldiers stopped, but at a safe distance. Rab was relieved to see them raise their spears to upright. He hoped that meant they no longer viewed him as a threat, at least not a severe one.

"We know who you are. What are you doing here?" the younger one demanded.

Before Rab could answer, the older asked, "What did you say?"

"I said I am glad to see you because I need your help," Rab answered evenly.

The two soldiers looked at each other then stared back at Rab. "Why would we help you?" the younger finally asked.

Rab could feel heat rising on the back of his neck, but kept his voice calm as he said, "You certainly don't have any reason to help me, but I need to speak to your commander. Will you take me to him?"

"What possible business do you …" the younger soldier began, but was cut off by the older who asked "Are you certain the Centurion wants to see you?"

Rab was relieved to hear that the officer was still in the city. "Honestly, no I am not certain," Rab began trying to be agreeable, but then added, "but he might want to make that decision. Don't you think?"

The two looked at each other. The older finally gave a slight nod of his head.

The younger soldier turned back to Rab, pointed toward the Praetorium and said, "He's over there. Go. We will follow you." Then he added, "Just give us one little excuse and it will be our pleasure to take care of you like we did your two pals."

Rab was glad the two were behind him and could not see his eyes squint and the muscles tighten in his jaws.

The three stopped in the courtyard in front of the Praetorium. The younger soldier stood at a distance watching Rab, while the older soldier went inside the Praetorium. Rab was silently studying the Pavement Stone. In his mind he could still hear the shouts of the mob. Shouts he had thought were aimed at him, "Crucify him! Crucify him!" Rab wiped his face with his sleeve and looked up at the late afternoon sun.

This may not have been such a good idea, he thought and was considering dismissing himself when the older soldier returned with the message that the Centurion would be out soon. He then instructed Rab to take a seat and pointed to the porch. All three climbed the steps. Rab was grateful for the shade as he sat down on a stone bench. The soldiers moved off near the door and waited. When the officer came out the older soldier pointed in Rab's direction. Rab watched as the officer dismissed the two soldiers and started toward him. Rab stood as the Centurion approached, but he could not read the older man's face. It was dark from years in the sun. Its many creases did not give any indication as to the man's disposition. He wore no helmet and Rab could see his hair had turned a silver grey.

"My soldiers told me you were here," the Centurion began. "I have been expecting you."

Rab could not hide his surprise. "Expecting me? Why would you be expecting me?" he managed to ask.

"First, are you armed," the officer asked.

Again Rab was taken back. "Why do you ask?" was all he could think to say.

"Besides the obvious?" the officer asked.

Rab nodded.

"I would like to talk with you in private, but safely just in case I am wrong about your motives," the Roman explained.

"Yes sir," Rab said.

"Yes, you understand, or Yes, you are armed," the

Centurion asked.

"Yes ... both," stammered Rab. "I always carry a small dagger." Rab could not believe he was actually confiding in this Roman.

"That's fine. It is a dangerous world, filled with thieves and other malcontents. It is good to be prepared to defend yourself," the officer said. "You can see that I too am prepared."

Rab had already noticed his left hand resting on the handle of the small officer's sword hanging from his belt. The Centurion's voice was calm, but his point was not lost on Rab who had to smile at the understanding they had reached.

As much as he hated to admit it, Rab liked the man who was now suggesting they sit down.

When both were seated the officer asked, "Now what can I do for you?"

"First, Sir," Rab began, "Why were you expecting me?"

"Well, maybe 'expecting' was a bit too much. Let's say I was not surprised," the officer said.

"Okay, not surprised," said Rab, "Why not?"

The officer explained, "Because your life has been turned upside down. Your gang, or friends, have been killed. You have just received an official pardon from all your many former misdeeds. If that were not enough you just witnessed first-hand what may prove to be a pivotal event in human history."

Rab listened carefully.

"You are now at a point in your own life of making some major decisions and you are searching for answers to help you make those decisions," the officer continued. "Am I close?"

Rab sat there stunned and surprised. Stunned because of how accurate this man was and surprised that the man was a Roman. All he could manage was to nod his head.

"Joshua Bar-Abbas ... Yes, I know your name ...

Your debt to society, maybe even to God, has been paid in full." The officer hit his right fist into the open palm of his left hand as if to stamp a document. "The opportunity for you to become a completely different kind of man is like a door standing wide open right in front of you. You can ignore it and go back to your old life-style, or you can dare to walk through the door and walk in a new way. It's up to you," he concluded.

Finally Rab spoke, "Are you saying that I am some kind of special person or something?"

"No, you are not special nor is the opportunity special. Everybody has the same opportunity every day that we are alive. But what has happened to you, and how it has happened, has made your opportunity to change so obvious. It is even obvious to me and I don't even know you well," he explained.

"What is obvious?" Rab asked needing clarification.

"What is obvious is that you are a thief and a murderer," the Centurion began.

Rab felt his blood run cold and his face get hot. He shifted uncomfortably.

"What is obvious is that Jesus of Nazareth paid your debt. He took your place on Skull Hill. When He was executed in your place He satisfied the laws of the Jewish nation and those of the Roman government. As far as Rome is concerned you are no longer guilty. You are an ordinary citizen. That's why my soldiers did not arrest you on sight."

There was no way Rab felt "not guilty", but it must be true at least with the laws of man; here he was sitting on the porch of the Praetorium chatting with the executioner of the Roman Governor. *But what about the other Governor?*

"What did you mean when you said my debt was paid? How did you put it, 'maybe even to God?'" Rab asked.

"Now we get down to it," the Centurion said smiling. "I guess I believe it is possible that Jesus of Nazareth was who His followers said He was."

"When He died I heard you say, 'Truly He was the Son of God.'" Rab interrupted. "Why did you say that?"

The Centurion looked around as if to make sure no one else was listening. He looked back at Rab and said, "You probably know that most Romans believe in a host of gods. In our culture, Zeus is the main god. Apollo is his son."

"Did you mean to say that Jesus was Apollo?" Rab asked.

"That may have been the meaning my soldiers have taken but," again he looked around, "that is not what I meant."

"Then what did you mean?" Rab leaned in closer.

The Centurion leaned in as well before he said, "I suppose you know that what I am about to say could be considered treason," he hesitated and then continued. "I meant that it has become obvious to me that Jesus of Nazareth is the Son of the one true God and He is the King of the Jews … and … He is the true King of all peoples everywhere … and … and … Jesus is my King." The Centurion was almost whispering now and when he finished he released a long breath and slumped back. "There, I said it," he concluded.

Rab sat in silence. Thoughts were racing through his mind. This Roman officer had just confessed allegiance to a Jewish King. *He is right. That could get him crucified. I could use it for blackmailing him if I ever need....* Rab shook his head to clear his mind. When he looked back at the Centurion he could see that the man had a puzzled look on his face.

"Have I made a mistake in telling you these things," the officer leaned forward and asked.

"No, no, I will not use this information against you," Rab promised, surprised at himself. "But I must know how you came to that conclusion."

The sun was getting low as the Centurion began telling Rab his story. It had begun shortly after his being assigned to Israel. It was his custom to learn about the countries where he was stationed, so when he arrived he immediately began to interview elders and read the history books they recommended. Many he talked with had referred to the prophecies. These spoke of a coming Messiah, even though there was not much consensus about when he would come and how.

When wild reports had started coming in from all over Israel of healings and miracles being performed by a young Jewish preacher from Nazareth named Jesus, the Centurion had been curious. When he had called people in to verify the accounts, all the eye witnesses he interviewed were credible. One of the tax collectors had left his lucrative business to become a follower. The Centurion went on to tell how he had brought in for questioning a man name Simon, who was a suspected Zealot. Simon had laid down his dagger when he had heard Jesus' teaching to "love your enemies."

One of Jesus' illustrations was aimed at the Roman law that said a soldier could require a Jew to carry his pack for a particular distance. According to Simon, Jesus had said, "Show love to the soldier by carrying it twice as far."

As he studied these reports it seemed that Jesus had no plans to become an earthly king who brought peace at the point of a sword, but rather one who promised peace of heart and mind. It had seemed to the Centurion that kings had conquered nations and had enslaved millions, but none had brought true peace. He had wondered if Jesus' way might be better. That seemed to be the case when another Centurion had told him how he had actually appealed to Jesus to heal his dying servant. Surprising the officer, Jesus had offered to come to his house, but the soldier who understood authority had believed that Jesus had all authority and could just command the sickness to leave. That is exactly what Jesus did, and the Centurion's servant was healed.

Another type of evidence, the Centurion said, was his interaction with Jesus Himself. Despite its cruelty the officer was ordered to carry out the scourging and crucifixion of

Jesus. "The way Jesus bore the indignities and pain was in contrast to any I have ever witnessed. It seemed as if He were on a mission and that he was in charge, not us. He even appeared to die when He chose and in peace."

Looking directly at Rab, the officer said, "You saw the darkened sky and felt the earthquake. I could draw no other conclusion: Truly, this is the Son of God - no, not Zeus, but the real God of Heaven."

Rab had hung on every word of the Centurion's story. He felt ashamed that he had lived his entire life around the ministry of Jesus but knew less about Him than this Roman. He felt like he needed to get away and think. He was about to excuse himself when he remembered the one other thing he came to learn.

"That's amazing. That is quite a story, particularly for a Roman," Rab said, hoping it did not come out wrong.

The officer laughed, "Yes, you are right. But it was not the end."

"There is more?"

"Yes, I was puzzled that the Son of God would allow Himself to die. And yes, He was dead. I made sure of that before I let His followers take His body. I was saddened by Jesus' death, but even more so because I could not figure it out. Then I learned that the Council members had requested a guard to seal Jesus' tomb. They said that Jesus had promised that after three days He would rise from the dead. They were afraid His followers would steal His body and say He rose. So Governor Pilate appointed a guard. The guard sealed the tomb and began their watches. On the first day of the week there was a lot of confusion about what happened, but one thing was sure, the body of Jesus was missing. The first report I got was that the soldiers all said they had fallen asleep at night and Jesus' followers had stolen His body. That did not ring true to me, for two reasons. First, it was just a dumb story. If they were asleep, how did they know who took the body and when?"

He laughed and then continued, "Second, Roman soldiers know if they loose a prisoner they will pay with the exact same punishment as that of the prisoner, in this case, death by crucifixion. So I pulled one of the soldiers aside and, on promise of not punishing him, asked him what really happened. In spite of his fear he said that early on the first day of the week a large man clothed in white and as bright as lightning appeared out of the sky and sat down on the large stone that sealed the tomb. When he did the earth shook and the stone rolled away. The soldier said that's all he remembered because he was so frightened he began to shake and passed out. He said the others must have done the same because when they came to, the tomb was open, and Jesus' body was gone. Instead of reporting in, they went to the religious leaders who bribed them to say they had fallen asleep at night and Jesus' followers had stolen His body while they slept."

"Now that story also sounds strange," the officer laughed, "except that it fits the facts better."

He paused and asked Rab, "Did you feel the earthquake?"

As the Centurion had been telling his story Rab had been trying to match it with his own observations in the garden that morning and had almost missed the officer's question.

As Rab nodded his head, the officer continued, "No Bar-Abbas, I am a Roman officer and have commanded hundreds of men in peacetime and war. I have seen a lot of men live and a lot die. I can honestly say that I have never heard of anyone who lived or died like Jesus of Nazareth. Furthermore I expect to hear reports from those who say He is alive again."

Rab thought back over his experience in the garden on that day and suddenly wondered if the man Mary Magdelena had thought was the gardener was actually Jesus, alive again. *Why didn't I think of that before? Oh! That's what the smile on her face was about.*

Rab thanked the officer and then, without thinking, blurted out, "Actually I may have seen Jesus alive." And then added, "I think."

The Centurion's eyebrows raised as he asked, "Really?"

"Yes, sir," Rab said, "but before I can tell you about it, I have to get some confirmation."

"I look forward to hearing all about it," the Centurion said, standing up and extending his right hand.

Rab looked at the Roman's hand, then stood up, took a step forward and shook it. He then turned and quickly left the Praetorium. The sun was just setting, but Rab hardly noticed. He was preoccupied with his hand.

Have I actually shaken the hand of a Roman soldier? What is happening to me?

Chapter Twenty-nine

The fact that Mary Magdelene's name kept coming up both excited and frightened Rab. The prospect of meeting her intensified both emotions. Rab knew she might be the one person who had actually seen Jesus alive. The fact that she was an attractive, well-off widow who was more or less his own age was another positive. On the other hand, she might recognize him as a thief and, despite his being pardoned of all old charges, she could make a lot of trouble for him if she decided to bring new ones.

But even if she does think I am the one who robbed her, would she not follow the teachings of Jesus and forgive? Rab wondered.

Under normal circumstances it would have been an interesting dilemma that Rab would have wanted to sleep on, but he was barely down the Praetorium steps before deciding to ask Joseph to introduce him to Magdelena.

Of course, Joseph can refuse, Rab considered, but he didn't think he would. Hopefully he could find out first thing in the morning.

Sleep did not come easy that night, but not for the usual reasons. Rab actually was thankful when the sun finally came up. After letting himself in the garden gate, Rab took the path that led to the working area of the garden. Not much was going on but pruning at this time of the year, and so it was possible Joseph might not be there. He was happy to find him sitting at a work bench and called out his name as soon as he got near enough.

Joseph turned around, let a huge smile take over his face and said, "Joshua, my boy, it is great to see you." Then motioning with both hands, he said, "Come on over here and let me look at you."

As Rab approached, the older man stood up, reached out his arms and gave the surprised Rab a big hug accompanied by vigorous slaps on his back. "Now sit down here and tell me what's on your mind," he said pointing to a stool.

Rab sat down and told Joseph of his meeting with the Centurion. From time to time, Joseph interrupted with questions, but for the most part listened intently. When Rab got to the part about the Centurion's confessing that Jesus was his King, he thought the old man was going to burst with enthusiasm. In fact, he jumped up and began to dance around.

"That is one of the greatest things I have ever heard," Joseph exclaimed. "You see, the Scriptures tell us that God made a promise to our father Abraham. If Abraham would trust Him, He would bless Abraham and then use Abraham to bless the whole world.

Rab must have looked confused because Joseph laughed, grabbed his stool, pulled it closer and said, "God didn't mean Abraham alone, though he was a blessed man, but through Abraham's offspring."

When Rab still didn't understand, Joseph explained, "You see Jesus is the promised offspring of Abraham. Jesus is the Messiah of the Jews, but he is also the source of blessing for people of every nation. In fact the same prophet whose writings encouraged me to prepare the tomb, also wrote that God's servant ... that's Jesus," Joseph said with a wink ... "would be a 'light to the nations so that salvation may reach to the end of the earth.'"

"So you're saying that ..."

"I'm not saying, Joshua. The Scriptures say," Joseph corrected.

"Okay, so you ... rather, the Scriptures say that Gentiles will be able to know God too?" Rab asked carefully.

"That's exactly right. What is happening with your Centurion friend shows that God is keeping His word."

It was startling for Rab to hear Joseph describe the Roman officer as his friend. He would have never believed that any Roman, much less a soldier would ever be his friend. *But I now think of Joseph a friend,* he considered, as he studied the older man who was chattering away. *I seem to have been making new friends, all among followers of Jesus.* The thought gave him courage to ask Joseph about Mary Magdelena.

"That is really great," Rab said trying to match Joseph's enthusiasm. Then after a pause he said, "Joseph, I need your help. You see the Centurion evidently believed in Jesus even before the reports of the empty tomb. Rab then told Joseph what the Centurion had said about the Roman guards, the seal on the stone, the big man dressed in white."

"I am sure that was an angel," Joseph explained. "I told you," he concluded with a grin.

"It's beginning to look that way," Rab conceded without trying to match Joseph's enthusiasm. "Anyway the Centurion also told me about the scheme between the soldiers and the priests."

Joseph's eyebrows lifted, but Rab noticed an almost imperceptible nod.

"The Centurion believes that Jesus has risen. Though he has not heard any eye-witnesses." Rab stopped to measure his words, then said, "I think it would be really important, as you suggested earlier, for me to talk with some people who actually saw Jesus after He was raised from the dead."

He didn't have to wait long for Joseph's reply. "My boy, how many would you like to meet?"

Rab was taken back. "Huh?"

"How many reports would you like to hear?"

Still noting the blank look on Joshua's face he continued, "The risen Jesus has already appeared to many of his followers. In fact, several were in a locked room on that first night and he appeared in the flesh in that room. Remember I told you there was a reason I believed Jesus did not need the stone moved from the entrance to get out of the tomb?"

Rab nodded.

"I still think you should hear that story first hand. And

there are others I can introduce you to who have seen Jesus alive. How does that sound to you?"

"Good ... great," Rab said, trying to match Joseph's enthusiasm. He then asked, "Who was the first person to see Him alive?"

Joseph thought a moment and then said, "That would be Mary Magdelene. She saw Jesus ..."

"You mean the risen Jesus showed Himself to a woman first," Rab asked, feigning ignorance. "In our culture, where women are not valued very highly, that would not have been my choice for the first witness," Rab protested.

"You are correct Joshua," Joseph agreed. "In fact the Romans won't even let women testify in court, but don't you see, that act alone demonstrates what I was talking about earlier. Through Jesus, God has torn down the barriers between Himself and man. Let me correct myself. I should say, mankind, because that includes women as well as men. It is wonderful," Joseph continued absolutely beaming. "It's genius that a woman was the first witness."

Rab watched as Joseph's eyes drifted upward and he seemed to be carried away in wonder. After a bit, Rab raised his hand to get Joseph's attention. He was about to ask about Mary Magdelene when the older man snapped out of his reverie.

"Wait!" Joseph almost shouted. "Would you like to meet Mary and hear her tell the story, herself?"

"Sure," Rab said. He didn't have to feign excitement at that idea.

"I think I can arrange that," Joseph said. "Have you had any breakfast?"

As Rab shook his head, Joseph continued, "I am such a terrible host. Please forgive me. You can eat while I go find Mary. I know she will be happy to tell you all about it."

Joseph quickly brought out some food, set a place at one of the work tables and then hurried up the path.

Rab ate slowly letting his mind drift back over the

events of the last few days. Certainly many of his long-held beliefs were being challenged. He was uncomfortable looking back over his life and knowing that he had made so many bad decisions. He knew he wanted ... needed a change. But he had tried in the past and failed.

Didn't I try to get a shop so I could quit being a thief?

That doesn't count, he told himself. *You were just going to rob people in an "honest" way.*

After finishing his meal in silence, he decided to walk around. The garden was in such great condition. It was in full bloom. As he looked at the trees and vines with their new blossoms it was obvious that much care and attention had gone into every plant.

Joseph really is an amazing man, Rab decided and then recalled the conversation about Mary. It had certainly worked out the way Rab had hoped. The thought of meeting her soon was exciting. He did want to hear her story, but he knew his motives were anything but pure.

Who am I kidding? I don't have any business being here. The only reason I am here is because I tried to steal some spices from those women. What am I doing here? Yeah, I'm going to meet Magdelena, but on false pretenses. Rab knew he had purposely manipulated Joseph.

I haven't even told him that I was in the garden on that first morning. I am such a deceiver. Will I never change my ways?

With new life bursting all around him, Rab felt totally out of place. Instead of bringing him joy, everything suddenly seemed to be in such contrast to his life of chaos and violence. He had just about decided to leave, to run, but then he glimpsed the tomb and decided to take one more look.

A jumble of thoughts ran through his mind as he walked toward the rock wall. He envied Joseph: his business accomplishments, his optimism and joy, his friendships, his faith in the Scriptures ... and in Jesus. That was the hard part.

Even if Jesus was the Messiah, would it make any difference in my life? Rab wondered. *Especially after the way I treated Him.*

Rab lowered his head and stepped into the tomb. Instantly coolness washed over his face. The dark gave way more gradually. Rab was not sure what he was looking for, maybe convincing proof that somehow all this mattered. *How can you even know for sure He is the Messiah?* Rab took a deep breath of the cool air and walked over to the burial shelves. Two were undisturbed, but there was a linen cloth lying along the third. To the side was another, smaller cloth. *This no doubt covered his head,* Rab thought observing that the blood stains seemed to match his memory of how Jesus was beaten…*and the crown of thorns.* That caused him to examine more closely the larger cloth. The top cloth was stained in a position that would have lined up with where the soldier had plunged in his spear. Lifting it up, Rab gasped. The cloth beneath had been fairly soaked in blood. *From the scourging and the work on the cross,* Rab decided.

"This certainly appears to be the real thing," Rab said quietly, his words echoing a little in the cave-like tomb. Rab laid the cloth back in place and looked around. A very strange feeling came over him. It was like there was something he was supposed to see, or to know.

"What is it?" he asked out loud. Rab was grateful that none of his friends, what were left of them, were present to hear what he thought might have been another prayer. It was cool in the tomb, but he felt warm. He wiped his brow with his sleeve and was about to leave when he knew the answer to his question.

The tomb is empty, he realized. Rab fingered the burial cloth again as he looked around. "He is not here," he said quietly as a shiver ran down his back.

Suddenly Rab felt very uncomfortable, like he was being called on to make a decision, about what he was not sure. He shook his head to clear his mind. He felt the need to leave and started toward the entrance, but something was trying to get his attention. Rab hesitated, looking around. It was the perfume. The sweet aroma had been beckoning him since he first came inside. He peered back at the shelf. He saw the remains of several different kinds of perfumes scattered along the shelf and on the floor. Shaken out of his stupor, he became a man with a purpose. He picked up a bit of the perfume, brought it up to his nose. *This is really good quality*, he decided, and using his hands, started scooping the remnants into piles. He was just looking for something to put the perfume in when he heard his name being called.

"Joshua, Joshua, where are you?"

Rab felt like he had the first time he'd been caught stealing fruit as a young boy - shame, trapped, his true motives discovered. However, this time added to the mix was anger, at himself, for even considering what he had been thinking of doing. *You're an idiot!*

He glanced at the sunlight pouring through the entrance. Seeing no one and no shadow, he quickly scattered the piles of perfume, dusted off the front of his robe, and as quietly as possible dusted his hands together. He stopped at the entrance of the tomb long enough to carefully wipe any excess perfume from his hands on the cool inside wall. He squinted his eyes hoping Joseph would think his hesitation was to allow his eyes time to adjust to the brightness.

Chapter Thirty

"There you are," Joseph said as Rab stepped into the sunlight.

Holding his arm above his head to shield his eyes, Rab looked in the direction of Joseph's voice. There was a person on each side of him. On his left was a woman; on his right, a man. Rab instantly recognized Mary Magdelene and lowered his arm in front of his face to hide his momentary blush. The other man, younger than himself, looked familiar as well, but Rab could not place him.

"Joshua, I want you to meet some very good friends of mine," Joseph said as he stepped toward Rab.

With his left hand, Rab quickly covered his mouth and nose. He held up his right hand to stop Joseph's approach. He then acted as if he were coughing. Joseph stopped in his tracts and said, "I hope you are not catching something."

Rab continued his brief coughing exercise but nodded his head to indicate his appreciation for the concern. The action had its intended effect in that the three kept their distance. When he finished his act, he mimicked a need to wash his hands. Joseph smiled and motioned for all to follow him. He took them over to the work area, and while everyone stood by, he poured some water in a basin and set it on the table. Rab smiled a thank you and quickly stepped up and washed his hands. He dried them on a cloth Joseph provided, and then turned to face the three who had been watching him in silence.

"I am sorry," Rab said. "I guess the cool of the tomb …"

"No need to apologize, my boy," Joseph cut him off. "Here are the people I wanted you to meet. I have told them all about you."

The last statement startled Rab and he looked at Joseph to discover more of his meaning. The fatherly expression on the older man's face did not betray anything but warmth, and so Rab turned to greet Joseph's guests.

"Joshua Bar-Abbas," Joseph said, "this is Mary Magdelene." She stepped forward, extended her hand. Rab took her hand gently in his, smiled and said, "It is good to meet you." Mary's smile was warm as she greeted him. She then stepped back.

Turning to the young man on his right, Joseph said, "This is John, the son of Zebedee. He and his brother, James, were fishermen from Capernaum. They, and Mary, are followers of Jesus."

John stepped forward and extended his hand, which Rab shook firmly. John said, "I saw you at the crucifixion. I am sorry for the loss of your friends." When he saw the puzzled look on Rab's face, he continued. "I had met Isaac at the Pool of Bethesda and thought he was doing well."

Recovering his composure Rab inquired, "So the story Isaac told of being healed by Jesus was true?"

"I assume Isaac told you his story," John began, then smiled. "Stories can be exaggerated, especially over time, but I can tell you what I saw, if you like."

Rab nodded his head.

"Why don't we all sit down," Joseph suggested and pulled the closest stool up to the work table. He motioned for Mary to sit down as Rab and John retrieved other stools.

When they were all seated, John began, "As he often did, Jesus had come to Jerusalem for one of the feasts. On this occasion, we followed him to the Pool of Bethesda. It seemed odd to me that he spoke to no one as he walked around those gathered there. It was as if he were looking for someone in particular. When he saw Isaac Jesus stopped and asked him if he wanted to get well. Isaac indicated he did, and so Jesus told him to pick up his bedroll and walk. Isaac did."

"How do you remember this so well?" Rab wanted to know.

John smiled and said, "First, as I said, I saw it with my own eyes, but of course I saw Jesus do many, many amazing things for people. However, that particular miracle stood out because, as it turned out, it was the beginning of the priest's hostility toward Jesus. From that time on they did all they could to stop Jesus, to find some reason to have Him arrested."

"Why would the priests be against Jesus for healing someone?" Rab asked.

"Good question," John said. "Jesus told Isaac to pick up his bedroll and walk. When he obeyed, he was working."

"Working," Rab asked, "what do you mean?"

"According to the priests, carrying your bed is work. Well, Jesus healed Isaac on the Sabbath," John explained.

"So that meant Isaac was working on the Sabbath," Rab replied beginning to nod his head in understanding. "He was breaking the law of the Sabbath."

"At least according to the priests," Joseph interjected. "You see, Joshua, God's original commandments were wisdom for us to live by. They protected us, from ourselves and from each other, and were to be a source of peace and joy. But over the years the ruling priests and their lawyers added thousands of their own laws to God's. They call them interpretations, but to them their rules are just as important as God's Ten Commandments. There are so many rules now, that it is impossible for anyone to keep all of them."

John added, "I was with Jesus for three years and the only times Jesus ever became angry were when he saw the religious leaders use their authority to hurt people. The harshest words He ever spoke were to the religious leaders who used their positions to put people in bondage rather than to bring them to God."

"And that's why they had Him killed?" asked Rab.

"That's one of the reasons," John agreed.

"And what were the others?" Rab asked.

"Well, I believe they were afraid of His popularity," said John.

"So they were jealous of Him?" Rab interrupted.

"There is no doubt about that," John began and then looked to Joseph. "What do you think?"

"I agree, they were jealous, but they were also terrified that His popularity would result in a revolt against the Romans. They feared that if that happened, the Romans would take away their authority, and a lot of bloodshed would occur," Joseph explained. "In fact, the High Priest had said that Jesus should die for the whole nation," Joseph said, then added, "but I don't think he really understood the significance of his words."

"What do you mean?" Rab asked.

"There was another factor at work," Joseph reminded them, "All of those men are responsible before God for the decisions they made, no doubt. However we must remember that Jesus was on a mission from God. He came to earth to die. His death, like His birth and life, fulfilled so many of the ancient prophecies. It was part of God's master plan. Jesus willingly did die for the nation … for all of us."

Rab admitted he still did not understand that concept. He was still trying to sort through his own feelings about Jesus. He had hated Jesus, at first. But he was becoming increasingly uncomfortable with that position, especially now that it put him in league with the priests, many of whom he knew were more crooked than he was. *Joseph certainly doesn't fit that mold, thankfully,* he thought looking at the older man.

Rab realized the group had been silent, waiting for his response, so he decided to get to the point, "So Jesus died and you brought Him to your tomb?"

"That is correct," Joseph replied.

"So where is His body?" Rab asked pointing to the tomb, "not to be blunt, but it is certainly not in there."

"You are correct about that, Joshua, He is not there, "Joseph began, "but John and Mary can tell you more about that." As he turned toward Mary, who had been listening to the conversation, Joseph continued, "I am sure John has more to report, but first, I think I should get us a little bit of refreshment. Then Mary can tell you her story. "How does sweet wine sound to you?"

They all nodded then waited as Joseph retrieved a sack of ground, dried grapes. After mixing the powder with water, he poured each of them a cup. "It will still be another month before grape harvest, but I think you will enjoy this," he said as he passed out the cups. "At least it's cold."

Rab was surprised at how sweet and refreshing the drink was. The only wine he knew was the fermented kind.

Joseph then nodded to Mary. With the attention turned to her, Rab's anxiety once more began to rise. Again he wondered if she would recognize him, either from the robbery, or more likely from the morning he followed her to the garden.

"First, let me say that I am happy to meet you, Joshua," Mary said. "It is always a treat to talk with someone who wants to know about our Lord."

Rab nodded slightly and smiled.

"But I must ask, 'Have we met before?' I know you were on Skull Hill, but I mean before, or maybe after that. You look somewhat familiar," she said.

"I do recall seeing you on Skull Hill," Rab began slowly, "and possibly we have seen one another on the street," he continued, trying to be as honest as he dare, "but we have never met, I am sure I would remember."

Mary studied him closely for what seemed a long time to Rab. She then shrugged her shoulders, smiled again and said, "No matter, it is good to meet you now and to tell you what I saw."

Rab masked the genuine relief he felt inside. He simply said, "Yes, please tell me all about that morning." As soon as the words left his mouth, Rab feared he had misspoken. *Has anyone said it was "morning?"*

Rab was certain he saw one of Mary's eyebrows raise slightly, but she did not challenge him. Instead she began her story. Like John she too had followed Jesus for several years and had seen Him perform many miracles. He had even set her free from seven tormenting demons, giving her a sense of peace she had not known before. Several months ago, He had begun to tell everyone that He was going to come to Jerusalem and be killed, but that He would rise from the dead.

"But for some reason," Mary shook her head, "I did not believe any of it would happen."

Seeing the puzzled look on Rab's face she explained, "Jesus had power over creation, over demons … over everything …"

"I personally saw Him walk on top of the Sea of Galilee," John interrupted. "On another occasion, in the middle of a huge storm, He simply told the waves to be at peace." He paused for effect, and then said, "and the wind immediately stopped and the clouds began to break up."

John then caught himself and said, "I'm sorry, Mary." Then turning again to Rab he said, "I could go on all day and all night telling you of the amazing works I have seen. But I'll stop."

"Jesus raised people from the dead," Mary continued. "It just did not seem possible that He would allow anyone to take His life. And in my mind, it did not seem necessary. Why would He? For what purpose?"

It looked to Rab that, with this last question, Mary had forgotten the rest of them and was questioning herself.

Mary looked around, as if gathering her thoughts and then said, "When Jesus died the way He did, I was crushed. I couldn't believe it happened. I began to question everything: Did He really heal all those people? Did He really feed five thousand people with two fish and five loaves of bread? Did He really raise Lazarus from the dead? Was He really the Son of God? I was in such shock it never even entered my mind that He would actually rise from the dead."

For a while Mary sat silent. Rab started to ask her why she came to the tomb, but realized that question would reveal he knew more than he had let on, so he asked, "But you came to the tomb, right?"

Shaken away from her inner thoughts, Mary looked at Rab and said, "Yes, we came to the tomb early on the day after the Sabbath."

"We?" Rab interrupted.

"Oh, I'm sorry," Mary replied, "two other women, also followers of Jesus, were with me."

Rab nodded with a smile, but felt like a liar.

"We came to the tomb, bringing spices to finish the burial process. You see, I knew that Joseph did not intend to use spices. He had told me that," she said looking at Joseph, "but I did not know that Nicodemus had come later and had brought spices. The women and I thought we should bring whatever we could find. It wasn't a lot, but it would have to do," she explained. "We wondered how we would move the huge stone that was over the door of the tomb."

"How did you move the stone," Rab asked.

"We didn't have to," Mary responded. "While we were on the way, there was a powerful earthquake. Do you remember?"

Rad nodded.

"When we got to the tomb we saw the stone was moved away from the doorway, but more than that," she said excitedly, "there was a huge angel sitting on the stone."

"An angel?" Rab asked.

"Yes. He looked like a man, except he was very large and his clothing was very bright."

When Rab did not respond, Mary continued, "He told us not to fear that Jesus had risen from the dead as He had said. Then the angel showed us inside the tomb. There was another angel inside, and together they told us to go and tell His other followers the good news. We ran to the house where they were staying." Nodding in John's direction, she continued "John and Peter, another disciple, came to the tomb to see for themselves. I came back too, but waited outside while they looked in. After they left I was ... well ... crying when I heard someone speak to me from behind. He asked me why I was crying and whom I was seeking."

It was obvious to Rab that Mary was still very emotional about this. "Please go on," he urged.

"I thought it was the gardener, so I asked him to tell me where he had laid Jesus' body. He then called my name." Again she paused as if reliving the experience. "I looked more closely and recognized Him."

"Jesus?" Rab asked.

"Yes, Jesus," Magadelena explained, holding back her emotions.

"What did you do?" Rab asked.

"I ran to Him, threw myself down before Him and began hugging His ankles," she said. "I could hardly believe it. It was Jesus, alive, alive, like He'd promised."

Now she allowed a huge smile to envelop her face. Rab recalled that same smile as she had run past Him in the garden.

"He told me to let go of Him because He had to ascend to the Father. He then instructed me to go tell His brothers. Though I did not want to leave Him, I immediately ran to find them to tell them I had seen the Lord. John can tell you his story," Mary continued, "but I am here as an eye-witness. I saw Him; Jesus is alive. You can tell that to the Centurion and anyone else you like."

Again she beamed with that beautiful smile.

"Where is he now? Have you seen Him since then?" Rab asked.

Sadly, Mary's smile faded some as she answered, "I don't know where He is now and no, I have not seen Him again. However, John has. Why don't you tell him your story," she said, turning to the young man.

Chapter Thirty-one

"As Mary said," John began, "I came to the tomb with Peter. I am younger and faster so I got here first but just couldn't go in. When he caught up, Peter went in and looked around, then I entered. I didn't see any angels, but when I noticed the linen cloths and how they were laid out, I remembered that Jesus told us He would arise, and…"

"You believed He was alive?" Rab said.

"I did," John answered. "Jesus had been telling us for months all of this would happen. He even quoted the Scriptures to us so that when it happened we would believe. Even so, I didn't believe it until I stood in the empty tomb and saw the empty grave clothes."

A shiver went down Rab's back as he remembered his own experience in the tomb.

"We spread the word and everyone gathered together that evening. In fact a couple of the men had left town that morning and had been walking on the road to Emmaus, when Jesus joined them. Like Mary, they did not recognize Him at first. When they did, He left them and they hurried back to the city to tell us about it."

John now paused and looked intently at Rab. When he was certain his words would be heard he said, "The fact is we were all afraid the officials would find out about our meeting and arrest us as well. We made sure all the doors were locked. It was an upper story room so we weren't worried about the windows. What happened next was amazing."

John paused, took a drink and then continued. "First we listened to the two men's stories. Then everyone started talking at once, when suddenly Jesus walked into the middle of the group."

"Where did He come from?" Rab asked incredulously.

"I don't know," John answered.

"You said the doors were locked, right?"

"Yes, that's right."

"Well how did He get into the room?"

"I don't know. He just did," John insisted.

Rab looked at Joseph who just smiled.

Suddenly Rab remembered something. Turning to Joseph, he said, "That's what you meant when you said the reason the angels, or the earthquake, moved the stone was so people could look in the tomb rather than for Jesus to get out. Right?"

Joseph added a nod to his smile.

"Hmm?" said Rab and then looked back at John.

John continued his story. "Jesus raised His hand and said, 'Be at peace.' When we got quiet He showed us the scars in His hands and His side. When we realized it was Jesus, we went crazy. It was amazing."

"So ... was He like a ghost?" Rab asked slowly, trying to find the right words.

"No," John answered. "His body was real. He said it was flesh and bone. In fact, He asked if we had anything to eat. When we gave Him a piece of fish, He ate it right in front of us."

"Flesh and bone; not flesh and blood?" Rab asked.

"That's right," John said.

Rab thought about this for a minute, then asked, "What happened next?"

"We just celebrated for a while, laughing, hugging Jesus and each other, slapping each other on the back.

Rab felt genuinely happy for John and the others, but could not help feeling sorry that he had never been in the kind of party that did not result in a hangover the next day.

John paused and then lowered his voice for emphasis. "Then Jesus calmed everyone down and said again, 'Be at Peace.' But this time He added ... ." John's voice got even quieter and his speech slowed. "'As the Father has sent me, I am sending you.' Then He walked around to each one of us and breathed on us and said 'Receive the Holy Spirit. If you forgive the sins of any, they have been forgiven.'"

As He listened to John's story, there was no doubt in Rab's mind that the young man believed every word he was saying. "Does that mean you guys can forgive sins?" Rab wanted to ask, but he was sure he did not want to get into a discussion about forgiveness, much less sin. Rab finally just asked, "So what happened then?"

"Joshua, I have to tell you," John said quietly and calmly, particularly for a young man, "the most amazing sense of peace came into me. It started deep on the inside and then seemed to fill my whole body. I'm telling you the truth, I felt like all my past sins and failures just washed away and I was brand new. Along with the peace was a deep sense of love - for Jesus, for God the Father, for all those guys in the room, for everybody. It was amazing, simply amazing."

When Rab didn't say anything, John continued, "Sounds crazy doesn't it? A room full of tough guys: fisherman, tax collectors, Zealots, all hugging each other and apologizing for being jerks. If anyone had been watching they would have thought we were crazy. But it was great."

Try as he might, it was impossible for Rab to fully understand the scene John had described. He finally sighed and opted for a safe question. "You got Zealots and tax collectors in the same group?" Rab asked skeptically.

"Yeah we do," John nodded.

Rab started shaking his head. "I'm sorry. I was trying to buy this stuff, but you're lying. Those guys hate each other. Everybody knows the tax collectors are turn-coat Jews who work for the Romans. Zealots wouldn't be in the same group, unless they were there to kill the tax collectors," Rab asserted.

Instead of getting defensive as Rab expected, John just nodded in agreement. "I know, that's the way it is in the world, but Jesus is bigger than all of that," John explained quietly. "Those guys had been together for a while and for the most part, they had laid down their hostilities just because of what Jesus taught. But that night, when Jesus gave us the Holy Spirit, and His peace, everything changed. We all realized that that is what we had been looking for all our lives."

Rab could not wrap his mind around that kind of change. He really needed to think about what John was saying so he simply asked again, "So, you're telling me that the Zealots and the tax collectors became friends?"

"More than friends," John said as he looked directly into Rab's eyes. "That night they became brothers."

It was hard for Rab to relate, having never had a brother. The closest relationships he had had were with other thieves like Jonah and Isaac. Even though they had been through some serious things together, what they mostly had in common were greed, common enemies and the need to survive. What John was describing sounded so impossible ... but so attractive.

"Simon, that's the Zealot," John explained, "and Matthew, the tax collector, hugged each other like they were long lost brothers who hadn't seen each other in years. I'm telling you, it was great. I even hugged my own brother, James," John concluded.

Trying to hold his envy in check, Rab asked, "Then what happened? What did Jesus do then?"

"I don't know," John answered with a smile.

When Rab did not smile back, John explained, "He just disappeared. Well," he corrected, "He said He would see us in Galilee and then He was gone."

"Gone? Disappeared? Just like that?" Rab asked holding up his two hands.

"Yes," John said, making the same sign, "just like that. One moment He was there in the room with us and the next moment He was gone."

Rab didn't know what to think of that. Finally he asked hesitantly, "So He is going to meet you in Galilee?"

"That's right," John replied.

"Can I come see Him?" Rab surprised himself, and as soon as He had said it wished he had not. He looked at John and then at Joseph. Both men looked at each other, definitely surprised by the request.

"Joshua, it is wonderful that you want to come with us, and it probably will be okay," Joseph began. "However, the truth is we are not very sure at this point what Jesus' intentions are."

Rab could not help but study Joseph's face for some signs of rejection, yet he saw nothing but concern.

"This is all new to us," John picked up, "and we don't really know what He wants from us who have been following Him for these years, much less anyone else."

Rab listened for some hint of superiority in the young man's voice; if it was there he could not detect it. Nonetheless he suddenly felt like an outsider, a wanna-be who had just invited himself to a party. He wanted to excuse himself, but before he could, Joseph spoke up.

"Listen Joshua, there is absolutely no doubt in my mind that Jesus would want to see you again. He came to earth to show us the Father's love and to make a way so that the rest of us can become true sons of God. He wants lots more sons, and I know He wants you to be one too," he concluded, then looked at John and Mary.

"Joseph is right," John said, "Jesus taught us from the beginning to reach out to others and bring them to Him. I know you will be welcome."

"Do you know who you're talking to?" Rab suddenly said, standing up and stepping away from the table. "How do you know that this Jesus, if He is alive, and if He is the Son of God, will want to have anything to do with me?"

Rab was beginning to feel something for these people, particularly, Joseph. It was a very unfamiliar emotion. A more familiar emotion, fear, suddenly took its place. The fear of them rejecting him instantly overpowered his logic. Before he even made a conscious decision, he did what he had done countless times in his life: He rejected them before they could reject him.

"I've got to go," he said hurriedly. "Thank you for meeting with me." He turned and started walking quickly up the path.

Joseph, John and Mary were still watching in stunned silence as he turned the corner.

"Don't be a stranger," Joseph hollered after him. "Joshua Bar-Abbas, you are always welcome here," were the last words Rab heard as he flung open the gate, stepped through and slammed it behind him.

Chapter Thirty-two

"What do you mean that God wants more sons?" Rab finally asked.

It had taken Rab three full days, and nights, to get up the courage to go back to the garden. He had told himself many times that he was a tough guy and that going to see an old man like Joseph carried absolutely no risk. Despite the self-talk, he sensed otherwise. He felt the old man and his friends possibly were onto something that could totally alter his life. Their lives certainly had been changed. The question was, "Did he want his life changed?"

That's pretty easy to answer. I not only want my life changed, I need my life changed. If I keep going on this path I am going to end up like Isaac and Jonah, a pile of bones in some ditch ... probably on Skull Hill.

Now sitting beside Joseph on the terrace, he felt better than he had the last two nights, with his "friends" in the tavern. Joseph had immediately welcomed him and seemed genuinely glad to see him. He had been more than willing to answer Rab's questions.

"We learn in the Scriptures the reason God created this entire world was to have a place for men to live. And the reason He created men is so we can become like His son and have a relationship with Him forever," Joseph had begun, then added, "That's why we are made "in God's image."

"In God's image? What does God look like?" Rab wanted to know.

Spurred on by Rab's quest for truth, Joseph replied, "There may be more, but so far I have learned that it is not so much our outward appearance as what we are on the inside," Joseph explained, but Rab interrupted, "What do you mean, on the inside?.

"What I mean is that though we live in a physical body and relate to a physical world, we are really spirit beings, like God. We are spirit beings and again, like God, we will live somewhere forever. Right now we live in these bodies. It also means that, like God, we are persons who can think, feel and make decisions. As persons we can enter into relationships, with others and with God.

"What does that have to do with our being sons of God?" Rab interrupted.

"That is what I am getting to. God doesn't want a long distance relationship with us. He wants to form us into the very likeness of his Son, Jesus, and have us live with Him in peace and joy throughout eternity."

"If God wants more sons why doesn't He just make them?" Rab asked.

"Joshua, that is a great question," Joseph replied. "Here's what I think. Some things are impossible, even for God. For example, even God can't dig a hole so big He can't fill it up. Right?"

Rab just looked at him. "What are you talking about?"

"Okay, that's not a great example," Joseph laughed. "How about this ... even God, who created the world cannot, or is wise enough not to, create us like Him and just drop us into heaven."

Rab looked confused.

Joseph noticed and tried to explain, "Right now there is perfect harmony and love in heaven among God the Father, God the Son and God the Spirit. That's because each honors the others completely; no vying for power or glory. Each serves the others with true love and humility. Every decision is made in perfect unity. That means there is no strife in heaven, just joy and peace. You might even call it Paradise."

When he heard the word, "Paradise," Rab looked past Joseph to Skull Hill and started thinking of his friend, Isaac and what Jesus had told him on the cross. *Is that what He meant, that Jesus was taking Isaac to Heaven? Seems like if Jesus was the Messiah it would be a mistake taking someone like Isaac to heaven. It sure wouldn't be Paradise with people like Isaac there. How does that work?* Rab wondered.

Joseph noticed that Joshua's mind appeared to have drifted off so he waited. When he had Joshua's attention again he continued. "Now remember I said that one of the ways we are made like God is that we can make decisions? And those decisions really matter. Of course some matter more than others. It would be crazy to put humans with so much potential for good ... and evil, directly into heaven. God knew that so He put us on earth so we could learn how to make right decisions, and so we could learn how to live in relationship with Him and with others.

"Kind of like an apprenticeship?" Rab asked. Rab considered that he had never been apprenticed in any real work, but he had heard discussions of it, and he had certainly been shown a few tricks of the thievery trade by some older than him. For an instant he recalled how the attention of older men, even thieves, had encouraged him. Now the memory began to awaken a too-familiar anger. He pushed it down by focusing on Joseph.

"That's right," Joseph said with an approving smile. "He also gave us laws describing His standards for our lives."

Again, Rab felt his temperature rising and he hoped Joseph was not going to ask him how well he was doing keeping God's laws. He was relieved when Joseph said, "The fact is not one of us makes the right decision every time. As for the laws, the real value of them is to show us where we fall short. One thing I like about the Scriptures is they are so honest. They tell it all, the bad along with the good. When you read the stories of even the leaders of God's people, you learn that all of them failed at one time or another, some of them miserably, most of them often."

Joseph paused to drive home his next point.

"Someday Joshua, you and I, every man and woman, will stand before our Creator and give an account for every decision we have ever made and every law we have ever broken."

Rab had been considering not only his life, but those

of his friends and acquaintances. He was quiet for a moment and then said, "If things are as you say and if God is just, He will have no choice but to lock everyone I know, myself included, out of heaven." After another moment of reflection he added, "It doesn't sound like God is doing very well in His plan of making more sons."

"It does look like that, Joshua. The entire story of God's dealing with mankind seems to be a terrible failure. In fact it got so bad at one point that God destroyed every living thing on the earth with a flood. He saved only one family and some animals."

"You're talking about Noah and the ark, right?" Rab had heard that story and had wondered if it was just a fable. Evidently Joseph thought it was true.

"That's right, but there have been many other examples of man's failure. It does seem like failure for God too, except for one thing. From the beginning He had a backup plan."

"A backup plan; what was God's backup plan?" Rab asked.

"I used to call it The Double," Joseph said with a slight twinkle in his eye."

"What do you mean, The Double?" Rab asked.

"I'll explain it in a minute," Joseph said, still smiling.

"But it is about Jesus, right? Jesus is the backup plan?" Rab asked. "Well that plan got messed up too when Jesus got arrested, beaten and crucified!"

"There's where you are wrong, Joshua. That was the plan," Joseph said.

Rab shook his head in confusion.

"It sounds desperate and it was, but you see, God planned from before creation to send His Son, Jesus to earth to live among us. In His life, His actions and words, He showed us the loving character of God. He is the only man who ever lived that did not fail. For that reason, He is the only person on earth who did not deserve to die," Joseph said.

"Let me tell you something. The members of the Council followed Jesus around for years, watching His every move and listening to His every word. On occasion they even sent people, smart people, to try to trap Him into saying or doing something wrong. After all that, at the trial the other night they had to use trumped up charges and bribed witnesses to convict Him. Even so, the Council could not find any factual reason to condemn Him. And after Pilate examined Jesus, he too said he could find no fault with Him. So when Jesus allowed the Council to arrest Him and the Romans to crucify Him, it was part of God's plan to pay the death penalty for every other man's failures," Joseph concluded.

"And that's why you said what Jesus did was for love and that I, of all people, should understand?" Rab asked.

"Yes."

"Because Jesus actually took my place on the cross and I was set free?" Rab questioned.

"Yes!" Joseph nodded. "Jesus was an actual substitute for you before Rome. He died in your place. But all of us are guilty before God and what Jesus did on the cross was to take all our places so that God can forgive all of us and set us free from the penalty of death."

Rab looked again at Skull Hill and asked, "So when Jesus said, 'Father, forgive them they don't know what they are doing,' He wasn't just talking about the men who were nailing him to cross?"

"That's it exactly. He was asking the Father to forgive every man who ever lived or ever would live," Joseph agreed.

"I suppose if Jesus is really God's son and He can forgive the very men who are murdering Him, then He could also forgive other murderers and thieves and swindlers," Rab wondered out-loud.

"And not just those who have actually done that, but the rest of us as well," Joseph said. "In fact in one sense all of us are murderers."

"I don't understand what you mean?" Rab said.

"I am not intending to make light of any horrible crime, like murder, but my point is that because Jesus' death on the cross was to pay the penalty for all our sins, in one sense all of us are guilty of putting Him on the cross. It is as if we drove the nails ourselves," Joseph explained. "We all need his forgiveness. We all need The Double."

"The Double? Rab asked. "We are back to that. I give up. What's 'The Double'?"

Joseph smiled his most radiant smile yet and said, "I told you that's the name I used to call God's plan."

"I don't understand," Rab said.

"There is a Scripture written by Isaiah the prophet where God is comforting his people by giving them double for all their sins," Joseph began.

"That doesn't sound comforting to me," Rab said.

"You're right. It does sound like God is saying we are going to receive twice as much sorrow for our sins as we deserve," Joseph began. "And our experience sure bears that out, doesn't it?"

"It sure has been true in my life," Rab confessed, surprising himself.

"Yes, I heard a man say once that sin will always take you further than you planned to go, keep you longer than you planned to stay and cost you more than you intended to pay."

"Is that what getting double for our sins means?" Rab asked again.

"There are Scriptures that use the term double to describe the multiplied sorrow that sin brings. But that is not so in this case," Joseph said. "As you realized, Joshua, that wouldn't be very comforting."

Rab nodded his head.

"In this verse God is using the word double in a different way. He is likening our sin to a debt we owe him."

"A debt?" Rab asked.

"Yes, every time we do something against His will, we are failing to give Him the honor and obedience that is due Him as God. That disobedience is recorded in our book in heaven as a debt."

"Are you telling me God has a record of every wrong thing I ... I mean ... we ... all of us have ever done?" Rab asked, feeling drops of perspiration on his brow as he considered how much evidence there must be against him. Though he felt he needed to understand what Joseph was telling him, something in him wanted to dodge the issue.

"What about the good things we do?" Rab asked. "Are they recorded too?"

"Yes," Joseph said.

"That's good, then our good deeds can cancel out our bad debts. Right?" Rab asked as he began to try to think of some good he had done, but was cut short by Joseph's reply.

"No, it doesn't work that way."

"I don't understand," Rab said.

"Remember what God's purpose and standard is. It is nothing less than a perfect son of God, living with and for him forever."

Rab thought about this a moment and then said, "So when we do right, we are simply doing what is expected."

"That's it exactly. We are supposed to love God with all our hearts, souls, mind and strength. When we do, we are living up to our design."

"But that doesn't get us extra to cover the times when we do not."

"Right again," Joseph said.

"Then I guess we are all debtors," Rab said, sighing.

"We are, and if eternal life is the plan God has for us, what is our fate if we miss his plan?" Joseph asked.

Rab tried to think of an alternative, but knew in his heart the obvious answer. Finally he replied, "Eternal death."

"That's right, Joshua, it breaks God's heart, but He cannot force people to love Him and to live with Him. Even more sad, is that all of us have failed Him and deserve death, eternal separation from God. We all deserve to be discarded like so much useless rubbish," Joseph explained.

The look on Joseph's face told Rab that he was entirely serious. Rab's mind went to Gehenna, the garbage dump of Jerusalem. Thinking of the stench of the rotting garbage ... and corpses, the constant swarms of flies, the many rats, and the ever smoldering fires, made him consider that it just might be an apt picture of hell. The thought that he deserved to be there forever made him shudder.

"That is why I say again that we all desperately need The Double," Joseph said. "Now let me explain The Double. There is a custom creditors have for dealing with a debtor who refuses to or cannot pay his debts. To prod him into paying, one of them will post a piece of parchment in the front of his house or place of business. Then he will write on it a list, for all to see, of all the debts owed. If the man owes other people, they too can come and add to the list of debts."

Rab was imagining how long a list he would have if all the people he had ever wronged actually did that to him. *How embarrassing would that be?*

Joseph then made it worse by adding, "As I said, God is keeping just such a list of all our debts to Him, but not just what we did or didn't do, but our thoughts and even the intentions of our hearts."

Suddenly Rab's mental list became so long he could not stand to think about it. Instead he found himself trying to shift the blame. "What about all those creeps who have done things to me?" he asked.

"Good question," Joseph smiled. "We'll get to the list you are keeping of the wrongs done to you, but let's see how God wants to deal with the list he is keeping on you, okay? And this is the good part, The Double. Let's say a very generous and wealthy person has compassion on the debtor and decides to pay off all his debts."

Rab pictured this in his mind and said, "He would come look at the list of debts, then he would go to each creditor and pay them what was owed."

"That's correct," Joseph agreed.

"That would be amazing," Rab said.

"Correct! Then what would he do?" Joseph asked.

Rab thought for a while and then said, "I don't know."

"He would go back to the list, fold it, or double it up and write on it, 'Paid in Full.'"

Rab closed his eyes to help him imagine the scene. He could see the long list of his debts being rolled up (too long just to double) and attached now so that none of the debts showed. In his mind's eye the only writing he could see now was 'Paid in Full.' Despite himself that made him smile.

"The person who paid all the debts would then sign his name."

Rab was stumped by this. He could not think of anyone he knew who would sign his list of debts. Suddenly he recalled the exchange with the Centurion when Rab tried to stop the soldiers from scourging Isaac. "I suppose you want to volunteer to take his place. What are friends for?"

Joseph interrupted Rab's throughts when he asked, Do you know why he would sign his name?"

Rab tried to think about Joseph's question, but couldn't get passed the fact he had not offered to pay Isaac's debt nor could he imagine anyone paying his debts and signing his name. Finally he just shook his head.

"So that any other creditor, past or future, who had not already been paid could come to him for payment," Joseph said with a great smile on his face. "That's called giving The Double."

Rab made himself focus on the picture Joseph was describing. He likened the relief that would come from receiving such an amazing gift to how he felt when he realized he had been released by Pilate. Now he thought how grateful he would be if someone paid all his debts and took the burden of his wrongs from him and gave him a new start. For a moment he forgot about Joseph, who just sat quietly. He was not sure how long he had been lost in thought, but a flush of embarrassment crossed Rab's face when he realized Joseph was watching him.

"Uh," he began awkwardly, trying to find words, "so you call God's backup plan The Double?"

"I used to," Joseph conceded. "Because that is exactly what God has done for us. He knew our debts to Him were so great that we could never repay them. So He sent his son Jesus to us. He took our debts upon Himself. He paid them in full by dying on the cross."

"So because of Jesus' death, God can forgive every person?" Rab asked.

"God has forgiven every person," Joseph corrected.

"Then every man has received The Double?" Rab asked expectantly.

"No, not exactly," replied Joseph.

"I don't understand," Rab said. "Didn't Jesus say, 'Father forgive them.'?"

"Yes he did."

"Did He pay for every man's debt of sin?"

"Yes, He did."

"Then isn't every man forgiven?"

"No!"

Rab shook his head in confusion.

"The key word is 'received.' God has offered forgiveness, The Double, to all men, but each man has to receive it for himself," Joseph explained.

Rab thought about this.

"You see, Joshua, even in this most important of decisions, God is not going to take away your responsibility to decide. It's up to you to receive forgiveness. Your debts have all been paid, but you have to receive The Double for yourself."

"How do I do that?" Rab asked quietly.

"First you have to decide you want to end your rebellion against God and choose to live your life according to God's terms and not yours," Joseph said.

Rab had to admit he not only had rebelled against the hated Romans, but whether in ignorance or stupidity, he had also rebelled against God. His heart had become so evil. He had hurt so many. He bowed his head, sensing the weight of his guilt.

Joseph continued, "Then you just ask for it."

As Rab sat in silence, the realization that he was at a turning point in his life began to force itself into his consciousness. He became afraid; afraid that what Joseph said was not true, but just as afraid that it was. If it was true then he had a big decision to make. Something in him made him want to run, to escape from Joseph and this place. But he had never known any peace except in this garden. And he knew the peace was more from Joseph and his friends than the flowering plants. *Besides where would I go? All of my plans and strategies have led me to the brink of death on ... Skull Hill.* He looked once more across the way. The crosses were empty, save the sign. They seemed to be beckoning him, mocking him, "You're next!" He looked down at his hands and sat quietly while the battle raged within. He looked back at Skull Hill and then at Joseph and finally said, "I don't know what to say. Will you help me?"

"Sure, just start by telling God that you know you are a sinner and that your debt is too great to pay. Then tell God you believe Jesus is his Son and that he died on the cross to pay your debt. Ask God if He will apply Jesus' payment of death to your debt and forgive you. Then thank Him for forgiving you and declare to Him, 'Jesus is my Lord.'" After a brief pause, Joseph added, "It is not the exact words that are important, but the intention of your heart."

Rab listened carefully to all that Joseph told him. After a moment he quietly asked, "Do I need to get down on my knees or something?"

"It is not necessary, but you can if you like," Joseph explained.

"I have never bowed my knee to anyone," Rab began.

"I have been my own lord and at war with everyone, especially God."

Joseph did not say anything.

Rab knew he was being confronted with a life-altering decision. He thought back to when he had been shackled across from Jesus in Caiphas' prison. When he had learned of Jesus' identity, he had immediately decided to hate him. Even so, Jesus had returned Rab's scowls with concern and compassion. Jesus had literally taken his place on that cross Rab knew. He stared across the way at the cross. As if seeing it for the first time, he now noticed the dark crimson stains of Jesus' blood on it.

That should have been my blood!

Joseph's explanations made sense. The fact that Jesus had obeyed His Father's wishes and chosen to be crucified for every man, but especially in his place was pushing away an entire life-time of reasons to ignore, resist, even hate God.

"Maybe it's time I did that," Rab finally decided and slipped off the bench onto his knees. Haltingly at first, and then with more intensity he expressed his heart to God, acknowledging his sin and asking for forgiveness. When he could think of nothing more to say, he thanked God for hearing him and then declared, "Jesus is my Lord."

He knelt there for a while just enjoying a new sense of peace. After a while he looked up at Joseph who had been sitting quietly beside him. He closed his eyes and for a few more moments just enjoyed the sense of peace. In his mind he could still see the list of his sin debts, rolled up. He could also see the words, 'Paid in Full,' but now he saw, written in blood red, the name Jesus. He stayed on his knees for a while as the sense of peace grew in his heart.

Finally, he got up and sat down on the bench. Again his gaze turned across the way to Skull Hill. There on the center cross was the sign, "Jesus of Nazareth. The King of the Jews!" A tear formed in his eye as he said, barely audibly, "Jesus, You are my King now."

As he sat and looked at the cross, in his mind's eye he saw the sign change to read, "Paid in Full, Jesus." He made the decision to not fight the tears.

He couldn't remember the last time he had cried, but these were not tears of grief, but tears of joy.

Joseph saw the change in Joshua's countenance and quietly, but loud enough for Joshua to hear, thanked God for his new brother.

Rab waited until Joseph was finished and then thanked him for his help. Joseph smiled in return.

Rab then said, "That's The Double?"

"That is it!" Joseph said.

"But I didn't make a list of my debts or sins?"

"No, you don't have to do that because God has the list already made," Joseph said. "But his list has already been doubled and on it is written in Jesus' blood …"

"Paid in Full," they both said at once.

"That's right," Joseph said confidently. "But if you ever have trouble believing you are forgiven for some particular sins, you can make a list and present it to God and thank Him for forgiving you for each one."

"I see why you used to call God's back-up plan The Double," Rab said and then thought for a moment. "What do you call it now?"

Joseph pointed over to Skull Hill. "Do you see that cross over there with the sign with Jesus' name on it?"

Rab had barely taken his eyes off of it. "Yes," he said, "The cross that I deserved."

"The cross we all deserved," Joseph corrected with a smile. "Well imagine that the lists of your sins … and mine were written out and nailed to that cross," Joseph continued.

The joy at the thought of being free from guilt was growing by the moment and so it was easy for Rab to picture his list of sins hidden behind the name of Jesus, nailed to that cross.

"So now I call God's plan …"

"The Double Cross," they said together.
And then they laughed.

Chapter Thirty-three

For the next several days Rab enjoyed, and even reveled in, the lightness of his mood. He decided to go across town to his own house to see if his mood shift was genuine, or simply the result of spending time with Joseph in the peacefulness of the garden. He did not have words to describe his feelings, but that did not deter him from enjoying them. An added bonus was that even the Roman soldiers he would meet on the street from time to time simply treated him like an ordinary person.

He actually felt like a new man. He recalled Joseph thanking God for him and calling him his "new brother."

How can I be his brother if we don't have the same father or mother? Rab wondered.

Certainly, something very important had taken place and Rab decided he needed to understand it better.

He enjoyed the beautiful, warm, spring day as he walked back across town to the garden. He went through the gate and began calling for Joseph. Almost immediately, he heard Joseph calling, "Is that you Joshua?"

Before Rab could respond, Joseph stepped out from among the vines, hurried quickly over to Rab, and with a big smile on his face said, "I'm glad you're back. It's great to see you." Then he stuck out his right hand.

When Rab took his hand to shake it, Joseph squeezed his hand and then pulled Rab to himself and gave him a warm embrace, slapping him on the back with his left hand.

Rab was as surprised by his own joy at seeing Joseph as he was at Joseph's joy at seeing him. He returned the embrace and even slapped Joseph on the back a few times.

"How have you been?" Joseph asked as he pointed the way back toward the steps up to the terrace.

"Actually, I have been better than I can ever recall," Rab said, restraining himself from bounding up the steps. Reaching the top he went over and sat down on the bench.

"I still am at peace, at least for the most part."

"Well, I am really glad to hear that," Joseph said as he sat down on the bench beside Rab, "but you sound a little troubled. Is there something you want to talk about?"

"Actually there is," Rab began a little hesitantly and then paused as he gazed over at Skull Hill. He noticed that the crosses were still in place and he was immediately saddened by the thought of his friends, Isaac and Jonah. His mood lightened some as he focused on the center cross.

"That should have been mine," he whispered.

"Mine too!" Joseph said quietly, nodding in agreement.

Rab stirred himself, turned to Joseph and said, "First, I want to thank you for all of your help. I do feel much better. In fact, I almost feel like a new man, if that were possible."

Joseph interrupted, "Joshua, not only is it possible, it is a fact. You are a new man! You have been born again."

When Rab heard that he turned to look directly at Joseph and asked, "What do you mean, 'born again?'"

"Yes, that's a term you don't hear every day, but it is an accurate way to express what has happened to you, rather, us," Joseph began. He paused a minute and then added, "In fact that is the way Jesus himself described our experience."

"Did he say that to you?" Rab asked.

"No, he actually said it to a colleague of mine, one of the other members of the Council," Joseph said. "I'm pretty sure that I mentioned him to you before. His name is Nicodemus."

Rab thought for a moment and then said, "Yes, I think I remember your mentioning him."

Joseph said, "Well, he said he is going to drop by today. I think it would be best if you asked him yourself."

Rab thought about Joseph's suggestion. *Do I really want to meet another member of the Council?*

"Good timing, Joseph said with a smile, "He should be here soon. Let's go down and get some water to drink and maybe something to eat while we wait for him to come."

Both men stood up, walked down the steps and started down the path toward the empty tomb. When they reached the work area, Joseph motioned for Rab to sit down at one of the work tables. Rab had just sat down when they both heard a loud knock on the gate.

"Joseph. Joseph, are you here?" a man called out.

"Yes, I'm here. Come on down. We're here waiting for you," Joseph said.

"We, who is with you?" the man asked as he came down the path.

Rab quickly stood up and watched as Joseph reached out his hands to greet his friend. They embraced warmly and then Joseph turned around and pointing to Rab, said, "This is my new friend, Joshua Bar-Abbas."

Rab noticed that the man could not conceal the look of surprise that immediately came on his face, but the man smiled, stepped toward Rab and extended his hand. As Rab extended his hand, Joseph said, "This is my friend Nicodemus."

"My friends call me Nick," the man said, "except for Joseph," he added with a smile.

"My friends call me Rab ... except for Joseph."

Both men laughed.

"We were just getting ready to have some water. Would you like me to get you a cup?" Joseph asked.

"That would be great. It's beginning to warm up, but it is a bit cooler here in the garden," Nick said.

While Joseph stepped away, Nick spoke to Rab.

"I'm sure you saw the look on my face when you were introduced," he began, "I didn't mean any disrespect. It was simply one of surprise."

"Think nothing of it," Rab said with a smile, "I would have been surprised if you hadn't been surprised. Actually, no one is more surprised than I am. If you had asked me a few days ago if I would be sitting here in the cool of this garden with two members of the High Priest's Council, I would have said, 'That will never happen!"

"Tell me what did happen," Nick said as he sat down at the table and motioned for Rab to join him.

"I'm not sure where to start," Rab began.

Nick said, "I have a question. Have you met Jesus?"

As Rab began to nod his head, Nick continued, "How did you meet Him?"

Rab thought a minute and then said, "I'll be happy to tell you about that, but it will take a while."

"I look forward to hearing it, but let me ask a different question. Has He changed your life?"

Just then Joseph came back with the water. He handed each man a cup and then sat down. It was obvious that he had heard Nick's question as he turned to hear how Rab would answer it.

"Well, actually," Rab began, "That's why I came by today to see Joseph. With his help and guidance, I came to believe that Jesus is truly the Son of God and that He died on the cross to pay the penalty for our sins. Joseph also helped me to actually confess that I was a sinner. I asked Jesus to forgive me and then I asked Him to be my Lord."

"That's wonderful," Nick said with a big smile.

Rab continued. "Yes, my life has definitely changed for the better. I have had more peace than I thought possible."

Then after a brief moment of hesitation, he continued, "But I do have a question," he said looking first at Nick and then turning toward Joseph.

Both men nodded for him to continue.

"Joseph you said that I had been 'born again.' What exactly does that mean?"

"That's a great question, Joshua," Joseph began, "I'm so glad Nicodemus is here because he is just the man to explain that to you." With that he nodded to his friend, indicating for him to talk.

"I probably should put this into context," Nick began, "It was early in the public ministry of Jesus when He came here to Jerusalem for one of the feasts. The first thing He did was go to the temple. When he saw it filled with merchants selling oxen, sheep and doves and money changers taking advantage of those who had come to worship, He started turning over the money changers' tables. Then He took ropes and drove the sellers and their animals out of the temple. Word got around pretty fast about Him."

Rab was listening intently. He did not recall Jesus doing that, but given Rab's view of how corrupt those merchants were, his admiration for Jesus took another step forward.

Nick continued, "In addition, we started hearing of the many healings and miracles Jesus was doing. Despite the fact that a lot of our colleagues thought He was a fake, I began to think He might just be the promised Messiah. I knew I had to check Him out for myself."

After a brief pause, he continued, "Now I didn't know how the conversation would go, and I didn't want to have to face criticism from my colleagues, so I decided to meet Jesus at night when no one else was around."

That was pretty smart, Rab thought.

"When we met, the first thing I did was tell Him that we knew He was from God. I was totally surprised by His response. He said, 'Truly, truly, I say to you, unless one is born again he cannot see the kingdom of God.'"

"Well, that confused me so I asked Him, 'How can a grown man enter into his mother's womb and be born again?' Jesus explained to me that there are two types of birth. One is physical or flesh or born of water. The other is spiritual or born of the Spirit."

Rab looked over at Joseph and asked, "You said that we are made in God's image and that part of that means that we are spirits living in these physical bodies. Did I remember that right?"

Joseph began to nod his head, but it was Nick who spoke out, "That's exactly right, Rab, we are all born in the image of God, but when we receive Jesus as our personal Savior, He gives us His own Spirit to come and live within us, with our spirit, and we are…

"Born again!" Nick and Joseph said at the same time, both looking at Rab as they nodded in agreement.

Rab thought about this for a minute and then asked, "So, now that we have God's Spirit living in us, does that make us sons of God?"

"Yes!" Nick said with a nod. "We are now sons of God and God is now our Father."

As Rab considered that he began to feel something stirring deep within. Then the thought came to him. *I've never known my earthly father, but because of Jesus, I now have a Heavenly Father. I am no longer an orphan.*

His gratitude for Jesus growing, he then stated, "We are now members of the family of God and Jesus is our Brother!"

"Exactly!" Nick said with a big smile on his face.

"And that makes us brothers too!" Joseph added as he extended his hands, one toward each of the two men. Rab and Nick each took the hand of Joseph and then looked at each other and reached over and joined their hands, creating an unbroken circle. Looking at each other, one said, "Welcome to the family!" Then another said it, and then the third. Smiling, they all nodded.

Releasing their hands, all three leaned back and sat quietly for a few minutes. Then Rab looked at Nick and said, "Thank you for telling me that. It really helps."

"It is my pleasure," Nick said.

Rab said, "You know there is so much I need to learn."

"We all have a lot to learn," Joseph said as Nick nodded. "Maybe we can get together with some of the other followers of Jesus and see if they will help us."

"Great idea!" Nick said. Then looking at Rab, he added, "Jesus told me several other really important things, but one really stood out to me. Would you like to hear it now?"

"Absolutely!"

"Okay, here it is, word for word, 'For God so loved the world, that He gave His only begotten Son, that whoever believes in Him shall not perish, but have everlasting life.'"

Rab looked from Nick to Joseph and then said, "That really sums it all up, doesn't it?"

"Yes it does," Joseph agreed. "Maybe we should put that to memory."

"That will be a first for me, but it's a good idea!" Rab said.

"Well maybe I can find some parchment and write it out for you," Nick said.

"That would help a lot," Rab said, looking over at Joseph who was nodding in agreement.

"Listen guys, I really appreciate all of your help," Rab said. "I know you have some things to do so I will get going in a minute, but if it's OK, I have one more question."

Joseph and Nicodemus looked at each other, nodded and looked back at Rab.

"Thanks," Rab began. "As I said, I have had a tremendous amount of peace and I am so grateful for that. Unfortunately, it is not a total peace because I've been thinking some about all of the people I have harmed in my life before I met Jesus."

Rab paused to let his words sink in. Then he continued, "I know, Joseph, that we went through the process of listing my debts to God and I know Jesus doubled them and paid them all. I am at peace with God, but is there something I should be doing about the damage I have caused to people?"

"Well Joshua," Joseph began, "the very fact that you are concerned about that shows that Jesus has done a great work in your heart."

Nick said, "I agree with Joseph, but the fact that you bring it up also indicates that the Lord may want you to do something to clear your conscience." He paused a minute and then added, "You see having a clear conscience is a strong weapon that protects our heart, sort of like a breastplate."

"It also allows you to think more clearly," Joseph added, "and using the weapon analogy, it is like a helmet protecting you from further temptations."

"Well I definitely need all the protections I can get," Rab began, "I certainly don't want to get drawn back into my old lifestyle." Then after a pause, he asked, "What should I do to clear my conscience?"

"Here are some things that I have found helpful," Nick said. "First, get some papyrus and a pen, then get alone with God in a quiet place. Ask the Holy Spirit to bring to your mind every person that He wants you to go see. Make a list. Next, beside each person, write down the wrong action you took toward each one. Then beside each action write down the wrong attitude that motivated you. Now from that list make another list, this time placing them in the order of the worst offenses at the top then down to the least."

Nick could tell that Rab wanted to question this last step, so he added, "You will want to go to the worst first, because if you go to the least first, your conscience may begin to clear enough that you might just put off and never go to the most important ones."

Rab said, "OK, I understand."

"Once you have made your list, you will ask the Lord to give you the right opportunity to go back to each person. You will not have to force this, because God will open the doors to the people He wants you to see and at the right times." Nick paused, then added, "Now then you are ready to go back to each person."

"What do I say to them?" Rab asked.

"Well, first, you will ask if you can speak privately. Once you are alone with the person, you will say something like, 'The Lord has convicted me of an attitude of ……. toward you. You will fill in the blank. It will be something like anger, hatred, hostility, selfishness, disrespect… Use the word the Lord tells you."

Then you will say, "I have asked Him to forgive me and He has, now I want to ask, 'Will you forgive me?'"

"Then you wait for their response."

Nick paused to give Rab time to ask for clarification.

Rab thought for a moment and then asked, "What if they will not forgive me?"

"Good question," Nick said, "And there are several different reasons why they may not want to forgive. Some you will need to deal with and some you can't deal with.

"For example: If they do not believe you are sincere, they might say something like, 'It's not important.' Now your response has to be even more humble and you will have to say, 'It is important to me, will you forgive me, please?'

"If you are still put off it may be because deep inside they know that if they forgive you, they will have to admit that they have been wrong toward you and they do not want to go there. But you need to ask at least three times and if they still will not forgive you can simply say something like, 'I hope you will be able to forgive me sometime.'"

Joseph joined the conversation, "What often happens is the person will be willing to forgive and if he has wronged you he will also ask you to forgive him. When both of you forgive each other, you can establish a new, better relationship."

"I have stolen from a lot of people," Rab said with his head hanging low, "What if they want me to repay them?"

"First of all, I suggest that you don't admit to any particular action or crime, but stay with the attitude," Joseph began. "You can then agree that you do owe them and you can tell them that you are willing to work on repaying as much as you can to them."

Nick added, "You can ask them to be patient, but that with the Lord's help you will do the very best you can."

"That's right," Nick agreed, "Plus if they do not know Jesus as their Lord, you will likely have opportunities to tell them about your new faith in Jesus."

Rab was listening carefully, then asked, "How do I do that?"

"Good question," Nick said with a smile, "We want to make it as simple as possible. All of us who have had a real encounter with Jesus have three parts to our stories:

Our life before Jesus.

How we came to know Jesus and

The difference He has made in our lives."

Rab did not try to hide the frown that came on his face as he considered Nick's words.

"My life has been so bad," Rab began.

"Yes, I'm sure, Joshua," Joseph interjected, "but I think Nicodemus will agree that we don't have to get into great detail about our lives of sin."

"Right! We don't want to glorify sin," Nick said.

"This is pretty new for us too," Joseph added, "But I believe the Holy Spirit will have us speak about those areas that the person we are talking to will most easily relate."

"Yes," Nick said, "we are going to have to learn to listen and follow the leading of the Holy Spirit."

"And when we do, some of those we share with will want to pray to receive Jesus just as we have," Joseph said with a big smile.

Rab looked at Joseph and then at Nick and then said, "Thank you for taking this time with me. You have certainly given me a lot to think about. I do want to clear my conscience, and I definitely want to tell others what Jesus has done for me."

Rab stood up and reached out his hand to shake Nick's hand and then he turned to Joseph who shook his hand and said,

"Joshua, go and do as the Lord directs you and then come back and give us a report." Then he added, "You know you are always welcome here."

As Rab walked toward the gate Nick called after him, "And by all means we will want to meet together again."

Rab turned and waved at his two new brothers.

Even before he got to the gate Rab started asking the Lord to help him take the steps needed to clear his conscience. As he walked across town, he began making a mental list of those he had harmed. When he got home, the first thing he did was find a piece of parchment and began writing his list.

It was with a mixture of emotions that he did all of this. First, he was saddened by the damage he had caused to so many, but through it all, he was joyful that he was forgiven by the Lord and was free from that lifestyle.

Over the next days, when he wasn't working, Rab began to try to find the people on his list. Some he could not locate and he asked the Lord to help him with that. The ones he did get to speak to were usually surprised to hear what he had to say. They were even more surprised when, despite their push backs, Rab maintained a humble and respectful attitude. As a result, most forgave him, but even when some refused, he walked away feeling a deepened sense of relief and freedom.

It was a startling moment, when in the process of looking over his list he suddenly realized he had left off an important name, Mary Magdalene. He wrote her name down, then listed as his attitude toward her, "disrespect" and then beside that, "selfishness" and then beside that "dishonesty." Rab then asked the Lord to give him the right opportunity to meet with Mary.

He had felt drawn back over to Skull Hill and was standing on the street below it looking up at the crosses when he heard someone calling his name.

"Joshua, Joshua! Is that you, Joshua?"

He turned around and was surprised to see Mary Magdalene waving at him. She was standing beside the garden gate and appeared to be about to go inside.

Rab waved at her and then started walking toward her. He was pleased to notice that she was standing still, waiting on him. As he walked toward her Rab began rehearsing in his mind what he needed to say to her.

"It's good to see you, Joshua," Mary said to him as he approached.

"I'm glad to see you as well," Joshua began. "In fact, I have something I need to talk with you about."

Mary pushed the garden gate open and as she stepped inside, she motioned for Rab to follow her. He stepped in behind her and then closed the gate.

"Mary, if you don't mind can we go up to the benches?" Rab asked pointing to the stairs.

Mary turned, walked up the steps and then went over to the bench and sat down. Rab followed her and then sat down on a bench facing her.

As she watched him closely, Rab began to speak to her, "There's a lot about my life that you know. You know, for instance, that I was a thief, but there is a lot that you do not know. Fortunately, I have recently given my life to Jesus. I can say without hesitation that 'Jesus is my Lord!' I am learning how to obey Him in every aspect of my life."

Mary sat quietly, listening and nodding in agreement.

"One of the things the Lord has directed me to do is to go to people that I have wronged and seek their forgiveness."

At the word "wronged" Mary frowned, but she did not take her eyes off Rab.

Rab noticed the frown, and after a brief pause, he continued, "Your name is on my list. Thank you for hearing me."

Again, Mary nodded.

"Mary, the Lord has convicted me of three wrong attitudes toward you: disrespect, selfishness and dishonesty. I have asked the Lord to forgive me and he has. Now I want to ask, 'Will you forgive me for disrespecting you?'"

Mary looked intently at Rab and then said, "Yes, I forgive you."

Rab then asked, "Will you forgive me for being selfish?"

Mary frowned again, but said, "Yes, I forgive you."

Rab then asked, "Will you forgive me for being dishonest?"

Again, Mary said, "I forgive you."

After a long sigh of relief, Rab said, "Mary, thank you so much for forgiving me." Then he added, "If you ever want to know about the actions that came out of my attitudes, I will tell you about them and I will make right any harm I have caused you."

Mary smiled at Rab and said, "Thank you for that offer, but the fact is the Lord has forgiven me of so much that it actually brings joy to my heart to be able to wipe the slate clean for others so that we can begin a fresh, like-new relationship."

She then motioned for Rab to come and sit beside her on the bench. After he did, she pointed across the way to Skull Hill and said, "Our Lord has paid our sin debts and now we get to enjoy the benefits of…

Both stood up and pointed across the way, and then said together, "The Double Cross!"

Then both added, "Thank you, Jesus!"

They smiled at each other. They then looked up and, pointing toward heaven said, "Jesus is my Lord!"

Made in the USA
Monee, IL
24 May 2024